WHERE YOU FIND IT

Janice Galloway was born in Ayrshire. Her first novel, *The Trick is to Keep Breathing*, was published in 1990 and won the MIND/Allen Lane Book of the Year and was shortlisted for the Whitbread First Novel and Scottish First Book. The stage version has been performed at the Tron Theatre, Glasgow, the Harbourfront Festival, Toronto, and at the Royal Court in London. Her second book, *Blood*, a collection of stories, was published in 1992. A story from that collection won the *Cosmopolitan*/Perrier Short Story Award. Her second novel, *Foreign Parts*, won the 1994 McVitie's Prize. In 1994 she also won the E. M. Forster Award, presented by the American Academy of Arts and Letters. She lives in Glasgow.

by the same author

THE TRICK IS TO KEEP BREATHING
BLOOD (short stories)
FOREIGN PARTS

WHERE YOU FIND IT

JANICE GALLOWAY

JONATHAN CAPE
LONDON

First published 1996

1 3 5 7 9 10 8 6 4 2

© Janice Galloway 1996

Janice Galloway has asserted her right
under the Copyright, Designs and Patents Act, 1988
to be identified as the author of this work

First published in the United Kingdom in 1996 by Jonathan Cape,
Random House, 20 Vauxhall Bridge Road, London SW1V 2SA

Random House Australia (Pty) Limited
20 Alfred Street, Milsons Point, Sydney,
New South Wales 2061, Australia

Random House New Zealand Limited
18 Poland Road, Glenfield,
Auckland 10, New Zealand

Random House South Africa (Pty) Limited
PO Box 337, Bergvlei, 2012 South Africa

Random House UK Limited Reg. No. 954009

A CIP catalogue record for this book
is available from the British Library

Papers used by Random House UK Limited are natural,
recyclable products made from wood grown in sustainable forests.
The manufacturing processes conform to the environmental
regulations of the country of origin.

ISBN 0–224–04050–2

Typeset by Deltatype Ltd, Ellesmere Port, Cheshire
Printed and bound in Great Britain by
Mackays of Chatham PLC

*This one's for
Charles, Martin, Graeme,
B, K, D and R
and the man who was my father.*

'It is better to break one's heart than to do nothing with it.'

Margaret Kennedy

contents

acknowledgements

Versions of stories in this collection have appeared in:

Telling Stories 4, New Writing 3, Chapman, Vivid, Edinburgh Review Nos 82 & 93, *Radical Scotland, Original Prints 4* and on BBC Radios 3 and 4. 'Hope' is a developed version of a commission from the Institut Français.

further acknowledgements

Thanks to Cathie T for her commitment and bravery for having been my agent as well as my friend for the past five years; to Robin R for his continuing faith; and always, always to Peter K for starting me in this job at all.

valentine

I hate February.

There is no natural excitement about the second month of the year. Valentine's Day makes me embarrassed.

Despite me, the card is always there on the table when I get up, a boxful of something padded with hearts on the front and a poem that I scour with my eyes, trying to get below the surface and feel what it was that made him choose this one, which parts of it are closest to what he would say himself if he ever said things like that out loud. Only he doesn't. People don't, he says. That's what you buy the cards for.

> *You know that you will always be*
> *The one who's everything to me:*
> *Your eyes, your smiles, your heavenly touch,*
> *Mean, oh my darling, oh so much.*

Sometimes the poems don't rhyme.

> *One word is my essence of you . . . For ever.*

> *We two . . . are One.*

This morning the Valentine is roughly A4 size with a baby blue background and gold border, two rabbits on the front. The rabbits have inflated faces, cheeks all swollen up like they have mumps and the bandages fell off. You can tell one is a lady rabbit because she has longer eyelashes and a pink bow round her neck. He has buck teeth. Nonetheless, their whiskers intertwine. Inside, it says:

I never thought that life could be
As wonderful as this
You mark my hours with happiness
There's splendour in each kiss
And tho it's true I sometimes fail
To say what's really true
At least I have this special day
To tell you I love you

My eyes fill up.
They really do.

I watched a tv programme once about how they made movies. One of the sequences was about tear-jerkers, how they fix them up to get you weepy. They demonstrated by showing how even a really terrible script – about a couple on the verge of divorce, in this case – could have music and stuff added in such a way that you'd still get hooked: nomatter how implausible, banal or shitty the thing was, the programme claimed they could still make you fall for it. So I made up my mind while I was watching that I'd use the information the programme was giving me: I would see the devices and not be manipulated by them. I stared out the rising melodic line with plaintive oboe counterpoint, sat steely through a barrage of soft-focus rose-coloured filters, single tears glistening on flawless female cheeks and smirked at the swooping crescendo of synthesised strings. I could see how it all worked and was managing to be really world-weary

4

about it all. Then they did something hellish. Just when you thought you'd survived intact, a door behind the couple opened, flooding the foreground with white light and a child on crutches pushed himself forward out of the aura calling *daddy* in a tiny, reedy voice. It was ridiculous, of course. I saw it was ridiculous. Of course. But the bastards hadn't warned me it was coming. I just keeled over on the carpet and gret buckets.

Conditioning. Give me a cue and I play ball.

This is my valentine, the only one I get.
I kiss the first letter of his name, smudging the signature he has written in blue blue felt tip and underlined twice, imagining where his skin has traced over the card.

Blue marks on my lips in the bathroom mirror.
I stick the card on the top the tv before I go out to work.

Stella has heart-shaped sandwiches for lunch. She says she bought the cutter to make heart-shaped sandwiches as a surprise for Ross when he opened his piecebox and she thought she might as well cut her own like that while she was about it. She opens one out to let me see. Perfect pink hearts of ham, the grain of the muscle severed clean at the edges of bread. No butter. She is on a diet. For Ross. He told her she was getting fat. I imagine Ross in his factory, opening the piecebox she has prepared and trying to hide what he finds. If he can't hide it then he will talk about Stella as though she is stupid: tell the boys maybe not overtly, but tell them anyway what a liability she is, what an embarrassment. Some of the boys he explains to haven't shaved that morning. Others have tattoos. They're all glad it isn't them with the sandwich problem. Ross eats the sandwiches anyway, the shapes of the hearts hidden inside his hands, just enough to bite poking through. And the boys laugh, irrespective of deeper, more ambiguous emotions. Maybe they want their women to be as little girl cute as Stella. Maybe that's why they laugh, encourage Ross to do the same behind her back: they're worried their women don't love them enough to do something that bloody ridiculous. Stella looks up and asks me if I got a card. Her mascara is in blobs all along the bottom rim of lashes. Stella is hopeless with mascara.

Of course, I say.

Boxed?

I don't tell her I think it's a waste of money. She'll think I'm a killjoy or else I haven't got one and and I'm lying and being sour.

I've not had mine yet, she says. It'll be there when I get back with the roses. Yellow roses. Always gets me yellow. Romantic and just that wee bit different.

She sinks her teeth into the bread, shearing half-moons clean through the ham centre.

A big softie.

I suffer a sudden need to get out of there and brush my teeth. Otherwise I will walk around all afternoon with egg mayonnaise rising up the back of my throat like drain emissions. I leave trying not to hear the noise of chewing, Stella mashing her hearts to paste.

We leave work in a gaggle of five and squash into the same car. After twenty minutes or so, the tower-blocks poke into view. You can see ours from the road, blue towel hanging out the skylight. They drop me off and wave, glad of the extra space. I wave too till they're out of sight then start running. I run because I am wearing his jersey and need to get it back in the drawer before he comes home. If he finds out he gets moody and says I put his jerseys out of shape. He says I punch tits in the front, as though my breasts are leather darning mushrooms. I run up the stairs with the key on a keyring he brought me the week I moved in: tiny, delicate keyring with a white porcelain fob and my initial in gold filigree. I tried to keep it safe by leaving it in the drawer with my earrings but he got huffy. I bought you it to use Norma, he said. So I use it, knowing one day I'll have to tell him it's lost. The door doesn't feel secure when you open it: loose on the hinges. I keep meaning to do something about it but it causes bad feeling: if I pick up a hammer he thinks I'm trying to prove something. He's right. I'm trying to prove the door needs fixing but he won't buy that. He'd rather I asked him. He'd rather I nagged. Like his mother.

I'm always first back. Last out and first back. That means any mess that needs facing is how I left it so mine to clear up. Curtains not even drawn. On the way to open them I bump into the Moroccan table he carried all the way back from Fez which does not respond to cleaning as we know it, then reach and pull. Lots of stour on the sills and a clear view of the binstores for the whole block appear together. Over the binstores today, a flat stretch of sky is rising beyond the tops of the other buildings. Between the two furthest tips you see hills. Birds perch on the tv aerials before they wade back into the thick blue paste, settling on irregular air currents from the launderette vent. The polarising stuff in the window always makes the view look nice: bright and cheery. It's the thing I like best about the whole flat. I sometimes watch the clouds up here for hours. Not today though. Today I choose to tidy up. Behind my back, two out-of-date papers opened at the tv pages, a jar of brine with no olives left inside and an empty silver poke of posh crisps need cleaning. Chili with a dash of lemon flavour. Wee flecks, orange-dusted mosaic chips, tip out when I pick it up. I brush the slurry with the side of my hand, gather the debris. Share he said, we'll share. I get rid of the bits and take off his jersey with one hand, haring for the bedroom.

GET THEM OFF. YO. Catcalls and whistles. GET THEM BLOODY OFF DARLIN.

I'm in the bedroom waving his jersey out the window when I hear this yelling but it's only the guys from the bakery. They keep up the catcalls and I ignore them. We've done this umpteen times. No sign of the car. The jersey must look like a bloody flag, though. Maybe he wouldn't need to be this close to see it, a red rag, giving away my every move. But I wave the jersey out the window all the same, its scarlet sleeves catching and flicking bits of paint off the frame like giant dandruff while the guys whistle and roar some more. YO. I hope it will cool down and lose the smell of me. I don't know what I smell like but he says it's distinctive. He says he knows when I've been in a room. GET THEM OFF. I leave traces behind.

The immersion light goes on when I press the switch: dependable. It's an expensive way to heat water but at least this way there'll be plenty for him coming home, and if there's plenty of hot water he'll have a bath before he thinks of doing anything else. Like opening drawers and raking through his jerseys. He works in a glass office and sweats when it's sunny. That's all I know about what he does. That and the lunches: he always tells me what he's had in the canteen. Good grub, he says, subsidised. What stumps me is what else he does in there, what it looks like. I imagine a glass office, maybe slotted into the middle floor of five, him sitting at a drawing board and trying not to notice while the sweat burrows like insects through his armpits, the thick furze at his crotch. There are stains in ovals on his back and where the arm seams join. All the seams of his clothes seep. His tie is slewed to one side, top button on his shirt undone showing the hair at the base of his neck. Every so often he moves one leg behind the other, widening his knees to let his body breathe. His skin bristles with the slow movement of sweat beads. He frees the watch strap and rubs the damp wrist, goes back to what he was doing. Usually I imagine him holding a pen but I'm not sure what he's meant to be doing with it, what he's writing. Maybe he isn't. Maybe it's a pencil and he's drawing. I don't know what he does all day. When I ask him he says it's not interesting: he doesn't come home to talk about work. I know it involves pens though. He's never done pinching mine. Sometimes he's there from eight in the morning till after midnight. Whatever it is, it takes up lots of time.

Other times I imagine him walking along a sunned-out corridor, one hand balled into the right trouser pocket, jacket slung over the opposite shoulder, watching his feet as he walks. Occasionally, he kicks something on the floor that isn't there, a mimed football tackle that pulls back its power at the last minute. Just working off a little energy. When people go past in the corridor he nods and keeps going. Maybe he's going to the canteen and that's why he's so relaxed. The canteen has glass doors that slide back automatically when he's within inches of slamming against them but he doesn't flinch or slow down at all. He knows this place like the back of his

Oops.

Shirt on the floor. Didn't see it this morning.

I pick it up, breathe deep. His clothes are always nice to touch, aromatic because he's so clean. Even things he touches smell nice. I slip the jersey into the second drawer, shaking it a bit so the layers of things in there resettle. Mine are in the drawer above his. My things smell of deodorant. I shut the drawer and stick a tee-shirt on over the bra, then head for the kitchen. A half-eaten bit of toast I left on the work surface hits the bin, door to the still-open food cupboard slamming shut. At least tonight I don't have to think what to make out of two tins of tomatoes, pickles, anchovies and yards of herb jars. I don't need to think at all. We are going out. I'm just thinking it would be nice to sit down for five minutes, maybe make a cup of tea, enjoy the sun coming through the tee-shirt making goosepimples on my arms when for some unacccountable reason I turn round, zero back in on the living-room and find one more thing to tidy away. Another paper I missed first time round. I've been working all day but that's no excuse for sloppiness. Plenty of women work all day and have kids and a man to run. My mother tells me I don't know what tired is. So I pick it up: not consciously but something makes these decisions for you. I don't normally bother with newspapers but I read this. It says SUICIDE PACT FAILS. Underneath, a story about two pensioners who went out in a car, doused themselves in petrol then ran the thing into a wall at 60. They both survived. Not intact but breathing. Ten miles or so up the road to where I am sitting reading this. A kind of village with an open park and lots of trees. Ten miles up the fucking road.

The sound of car brakes shakes me free. Car brakes in the parking area six floors down. He's home.

I imagine him, winding up the nearside window and collecting his *Evening Times* from the empty passenger seat, reaching into the back for the jacket he'll dangle from one finger to come upstairs, sauntering with his eyes crunched up because his hair needs a cut. He'll be walking upstairs now with his eyes screwed small, maybe resting finger and thumb of one hand on either side of his nose, trying to shake off tiredness, happy to be back. My heart jumps when I hear the sound of footfalls coming closer and when he appears on top of the landing, all my nerve endings blister. I can't help it. I'm crazy about him. Wholly and terminally, raddled with love.

He appears and I smile, meaning it.
He walks in smiling back, presents spilling from under his arm.

I get flowers, something chocolate (usually heart-shaped) and a bottle of wine, dry white. The wine is a compromise. He prefers red: I prefer sweet but he can't bring himself to stroll into Thresher's and ask for that. He's got pals in there for godsake. Also the white is a tradition from the days we didn't know any better, the days we used to stay in and have lazy sex all night after we'd eaten my speciality with the packet of frozen prawns and strawberry mousse, a magazine recipe that claimed aphrodisiac properties though in a self-deprecating way so you knew not to take it too seriously. My only speciality. It recurs. The magazine page is spattered with pink bits, fatty blobs that show I have been that way before but I keep it all the same.

Not tonight though. I'm not cooking tonight.

I nod at his card, waiting on the sofa. He opens it while I watch, then sits it on the tv next to mine. They both threaten to fall off, not designed to sit upright: too full of satin and foam. Anyhow, he seems to like it. We kiss. The tips of our tongues touch.

I've not had time to wrap it, he says, fishing something else out of the poly bag. A flat, black box. I give him an oblong box covered with stars. We open them at what is meant to be the same time but I'm holding back. I know what he has since I bought it but I want to see his face. I'm just like Stella. He always looks the same when he opens something from me: pleased and shy. It lasts till he works out what the folded cotton really is. A pair of thermal drawers. He holds them flat in one hand, not wanting the legs to dangle, thin and empty, where I can see.

Very funny, he says.

I know something about the present has disappointed him. I interpret that he'd rather I was interested in what I've been given. Already I'm tearing the pale blue tissue, trying to rustle a lot so he knows I'm thrilled. One of the pieces between the layers touches my hand, soft enough to make my skin feel it's melting. I pull out something shiny, red nylon with a black panel, splay pieces on the settee. It's a suspender belt and bra, a pair of knickers trimmed with fluffy stuff, like tiny feather boas. Our faces look much the same then. Neither of us knows what to say. The evening is in jeopardy so we pretend this isn't the case at all, just float in separate directions and begin getting ready for going out. We haven't got all night.

The water is cool but okay. I fill my bath up to the mark he hasn't washed off after his and lie back, getting sad at the sounds of him getting ready elsewhere in the house. What he has to put up with, me being such a hard bitch and everything when he just bought me a present. After all, it's the thought that counts.

The fluffy stuff sticks to my skin cream. Two strands like ferns adhere to my upper thigh. I don't look in the mirror but it seems to fit as much as this sort of stuff ever does and the feather bits don't bumphle the material as much as you'd think. I dress fast, looking over my shoulder and listening, hoping to christ he doesn't come through. Maybe I want it to be a surprise.

The restaurant is somewhere we've been before: intimate concern run by two Italians with Scots accents. The waiter gives me the obligatory smile when he helps me to my seat, tells me I look nice and I smile back. Can't help it: I'm so bloody eager to please. He sits opposite, managing his own chair, and leans towards me in an anticipatory way. He likes good food. We get mildly drunk. Through the dessert and coffee we start sharing the looks that indicate sex. A particular kind of sex. I run my hand along the inside of his trouser leg with one hand under the table and he has to squirm while his brandy is being poured, barely able to stay seated while the erection forces a hump in his trousers. My hand shifts. Watching his face trying not to flicker when the waitress asks him if he enjoyed his strudel gives me a thrill of power. I'm making this difficulty, I'm altering his behaviour and it means he wants me. He wants me. I need to feel that's what it means.

On the way home, I hook the three-inch heel of one of my shoes onto the dashboard. He looks twice, undoes his fly as the car decelerates then stops the car and fucks me in a layby till the car windows run like rain on the inside.

I get more excited by this kind of display than I'd be prepared to admit when I'm sober.

Afterwards, I blush hauling my breasts back inside the feather and satin contraption, ashamed for something I can't quite pin down. He clears the inside of the windscreen with the back of his jacket sleeve and looks at me. I keep my eyes on the roof vinyl, listening. Sirens. I can hear sirens, far away like remembered noise, too distant to be definite. Maybe there's an accident someplace. I ask if he hears it and he says no. He says I imagine it and maybe I did. I get maudlin afterwards, volatile. It's what I'm like.

The parking space waits for us, a dry oblong on the wet concrete behind the Chinese. The launderette grille hangs on visible strands of condensation, dry ice. When we get out of the car, our breaths appear too, making low fog over the bonnet. There will be frost tonight. At the foot of our steps, I find an empty box and I fold it carefully for the bins rather than do it tomorrow. He doesn't notice these things. His collar flashes white semaphore from the top of the steps and I hear him reach for the keys. He opens our door and goes inside. This is our home, how we live. He is in there taking off the tie and loosening the trouser band, trying to feel relaxed. We have already had sex. Further touch is unlikely. I stall at the foot of the stairs, not wanting to, then hear his solution. Dirk Bogarde being earnest about something in a late-night movie. We always have the tv. Tonight it has cards on top.

And tho it's true I sometimes fail
To say what's really true
At least I have this special day

13

I can always go into the kitchen and make tea.

Up the stairs, my turn to lock us in for the night. The sound of actors speaking on tv, my heart bursting with wanting to give more, not knowing what it is, how to give it. And sirens. I hear the sirens he thinks are not there coming closer.

where you find it

Nobody kisses like Derek.

First sight you think he's got no mouth, just a dry slit in that dry sheet skin, lips that don't look like they'd sustain much at all, like worm husks, little worms rolled flat with no juice left in but you'd be wrong. When Derek kisses he opens his face so wide you think he's choking on something, like he's swallowing an apple or maybe there's one stuck in his neck, like he's bringing something up from somewhere deep and you open up too. You can't help it. He prises you apart like you're in the dentist's chair and you *know* you're being kissed. You know what he likes? He likes his tongue buried and moving around in there, foraging into all the available recesses. You can feel the wee cord that keeps his tongue on stretching, pulling up from the soft veiny mass on the floor of his mouth, tightening to its limit like it might uproot. That cord is in there all the time, folded up like a fin or stray slice of tissue left on a butcher's tray, like something loveless left over from ritual surgery and on most people that's how it stays. You'd never suspect. When Derek kisses, though, you get a share of everything, you get it all. Sometimes it's scary like there's an animal between us, an engorged mollusc trying to get out: other times it's like he's sucking me in, drawing me inside him so I can't breathe but manage. I never push him away. That reflex thing where you think you're going to throw up? Even if he pokes the back of my

17

throat, the bit that's sheer like a toad's belly, his tongue stiff as a nun's finger it just never happens because it's not that kind of thing, not like a punter sticking his dick there the way some of them do, some of them not even careful, not even bothered if it hurts or anything, not bothered about your vocal cords or anything it's not like that. It's wonderful, the way he wants you to feel all of him in there, the root of this other tongue with taste buds bristling studding up like braille saying I AM KISSING YOU NOW so I have to make room for my own interior, pressing myself out of the way and against his teeth, finding out the peach fur in the distant corners of his molars, my tongue-tip caressing the places no-one sees. I love that, love it, love knowing all his secrets, even those bits of him, bits he doesn't see. Bits he doesn't even know exist. I love having no option, no choice. When he lifts those big square hands out of the blue, tangles his fingers up in my hair and tugs so my neck tilts for him without my sayso and just injects himself, without warning, I get dizzy, sick, weak to my water. That he'll do it anywhere, even in the street just hold me, squeeze me like an orange and take what he needs; that he can't wait for me, he just can't wait at all. There's no woman wouldn't love that. Tell me there's a woman wouldn't love being wanted that way, a way that doesn't hide itself, a way that can't be shy. He doesn't want to fuck me. He doesn't even want to touch me anywhere else. Kisses are what I'm for he says. They're our thing, how he keeps me in line. I wouldn't let any other bastard do it, not even if they ask, not even if they're good looking or offer extra, I don't care. I'm all his. All Derek's. Good kissers don't grow on trees. It's worth bearing in mind. You don't get everything in this life, girl, count your blessings. Remember the things he can do with his mouth.

sonata form

A few stands, those coffins they put cellos in, the odd coat and sports bag. The flowers were there too but not him. She checked the wee toilet, the shower cubicle. No drips, nothing. It was just one of those things about being with Danny. People came and got him. They walked by the rank and file sticking their fiddles back in cases and zeroed in, even if he hadn't had time to wash yet, to change out of his soaking shirt. She'd seen him taking off his concert trousers, unpeeling the cloth off his legs, steaming like a horse and they just came in anyway, exchanging pleasantries as if he didn't need time to do even that by himself. She'd seen him zip hairs out by the roots doing himself up blind, maintaining eye-contact and a smile rather than say anything. Tongue biting. You had to do a lot of tongue biting in dressing rooms.

Over on the practice piano, two bus tickets, a chewed pencil. His teethmarks. Mona put it in her bag with the spare she'd brought in case he needed it then draped her coat over a chair-back, the shoulder-bag out of sight beneath it. No point carrying stuff you didn't need. His coat wasn't on the stool where it usually was. She looked around, scanning. It was there in an empty box in the corner, the tails junked on top with the lining showing. Crimson lining. Everybody else had grey but not Danny. You always found them no problem: in among all the other castoffs, Danny's tails were something else. Mona looked at them, the Ribena-coloured splash and black wings falling onto the

21

floor. At least the poor bugger had had time to change his jacket.
There would be women through there very disappointed. She went
over and fixed it so it wouldn't crease, smoothed the arms flat. A few
hundred quid's worth lying any old how. On the way out, she shut the
door carefully behind her.

After ten minutes of blind alleys and droopy paperchains it was
there like you couldn't miss it. People were spilling out the door,
trolleys of drink rolling in. Every so often, great baboon-howls about
nothing evident would roar out of the interior then fade. The second-
desk double bass and big blond guy who played the trumpet walked
in, doing their bit as players' reps. Some people actually liked it, Danny
said. They liked the free food, especially this time of year. Eric and
Simon were there too, hovering around the open door, peering in:
Simon with a bunch of something and Eric not wearing his specs.
They came sometimes but seeing them was always a surprise. Simon
turned then and saw her. They walked over with their arms wide,
smiling the same way. She knew they knew. You could tell by looking
at them. Simon rubbed his cheek against hers, gave her one of those
lightweight hugs he did. You just got used to them starting when they
were finished. They were good hugs anyway. She told them it was
great to see them and watched them go coy.

Well, she said, you got your money's worth. Was he great or was
he great?

Oh you, Eric said. He rolled his eyes. Never mind him.

No, Simon said. We want to talk about you.

Let's have a look at you then, Eric said. He held her out at arm's
length and looked meaningfully at her belly through the black frock.
They all did. There was nothing to see yet but they all did it anyway. It
was pleasantly embarrassing. Simon said he thought Danny was
playing great just for the record and they laughed. It helped. Another
few minutes of when's it due and how well she was looking. Things

were just starting to get easier when Simon braced up, looked down at his wrist. Sorry, he said. They had to rush, wouldn't come in this time: too much stuff to do, she knew how it was.

Ivor Novello for somebody's party, Eric said. But we need the money.

Simon stuck the bunch of flowers into her hand. Give the maestro our love, he said. And tell him these aren't his.

Mona cuddled them into the crook of an arm. Roses. Not for Danny. She didn't know what to say. They left walking backwards and blowing kisses. Mona watched them, waving, knowing they knew they wouldn't have gotten in anyway. Friends didn't. These dos weren't for musicians at all, not even the ones who'd been playing. She heard the main door batter back on its hinges, knew they were irretrievably gone. The draft made the corridor chilly. Her cardigan was back in the dressing room but she had no idea how to get back there. There was nothing else for it. She put the roses down carefully on an empty trolley, ran a hand over her stomach wishing it showed more and walked inside.

Danny was on the other side of the room holding a wine glass and an empty paper plate in the middle of a huddle of women. It was where he always was at these things, what he was always holding. She nodded to let him know not to stop what he was in the middle of and just took her time. Mona liked looking at Danny and you only got to look at somebody properly when they were distracted, not knowing you were watching. You got to read things they didn't necessarily know they were telling you. Right now, he looked that way he did when a concert was over and he thought he'd done ok. Self-conscious, shagged out and radiant. She knew that look from other places as well: it always meant something good. He was close now, close enough for familiar cosmetic smells to reach, a deodorant and aftershave cocktail. She reached for the plate from his hand without asking, took it over to the buffet table and stood in line with the men already there, loading up with fish and meat, lumps of mayonnaise-thick salad. Getting the nosh was Mona's thing: it gave her something to do. Cutlery in paper napkins, bowls, oval-shaped plates and glasses. Most of the table was glasses. The salmon had eyes in this time. It looked up at nothing, pink musculature in tatters.

Best bit eh?

A man with a tight tie reached past for a sheet of ham. A waitress with silver-coloured prong efforts was holding a slice out for him but he didn't seem to see her.

Best bit, he said. Where they wheel out the eats.

He rolled the ham into a tube, popped it into his mouth, offered her a plate then saw she had one already.

That's the girl, he said. He waved his fork in a cheery kind of way and strolled along to the next tray, chewing. The waitress still held the same bit of ham out but someone else got in first. Mona didn't want it anyway. She walked further up, found egg sandwich triangles, some cheese: the only vegetarian stuff that wasn't salad. They always had loads of salad at these things. Danny couldn't eat salad after concerts. It gave him the shits. He always had bad shits before concerts with the nerves and everything and it hung on. He probably wouldn't eat the sandwiches either but she would take a couple anyway. Just in case. She back-to-backed them on the plate, lifted a glass of something orange and picked her way back through. Danny wasn't looking in her direction but he didn't need to. His smile changed. It stayed in place for the woman Mona could only see the back of but it knew she was coming over.

Her son played, she was saying. Who knew maybe one day professionally she only wished she'd thought to let him come along you could have told him to stick in you don't mind if I call you Daniel. Then Mona got over and interrupted.

Hi, she said. She pushed the plate between them.

The woman with the son stepped back, followed the length of the arm to Mona's face.

This is Mona, Danny said.

Mona put her juice down on the table edge offered the freed hand for shaking. The woman with the son made a very big smile.

Lovely, she said. Lovely.

She didn't take the hand through. Some women didn't. Danny claimed his plate and looked hard at the shapes on it. Mona knew what he was thinking. He was thinking they never gave you real food at these things but not saying, pushing the triangles about with his eyes down. Mona let her arm drop, picked up the glass again. She smiled too.

So, she said. Enjoy the concert?

My goodness yes, she said. Yes yes. Who wouldn't have?

Mona nodded.

I was just saying to Daniel here I'm *such* an admirer.

It was said for Danny to hear and he knew. He'd seen it coming and turned away just in time. A woman in a black strapless thing who'd been waiting for just that moment had got him as soon as he'd shifted his footing. Mona and the woman with the son looked at each other again. The woman coughed, looked at her empty glass, back at Mona.

Sorry, she said. Heather. She almost pointed at herself, thought better of it. I don't know who you are.

Mona, Mona said.

Of course, she said. Of course. And you're . . . are you a fan too?

No, no. Mona was no good at this kind of thing. She could hear herself being no good at it. I just live with him.

Oh, Heather said. The hand without the glass fluttered up to her neck. I should have known, shouldn't I?

No you shouldn't, Mona said.

I didn't even know he was married. Just didn't occur.

He's not, Mona said. He isn't.

Sorry?'

Married. We're not married.

Yes, she said. A studious looked crossed over her face. I see. It must be lovely anyway. She turned and smiled at someone over her shoulder. Jean?

She looked behind her. Three women looked up. The two talking to Danny didn't.

Jean? It was louder this time. There's someone you have to meet here. Come over. Come and meet . . . um . . .

Mona, Mona said.

Daniel's wife, Heather said.

All three came over. Mona held out her hand again. Two responded this time. Mona said her name to each of them to be on the safe side. She had to ask theirs. Jean, Carolyn, Stephanie, they said. They all had lovely teeth.

You must be very proud, Jean said.

I know I would be, said Carolyn.

Oh yes, Mona said, very proud.

He plays so beautifully. We were just saying, weren't we, girls? Jean opened her eyes wide to take them all in. Just saying we could listen all night.

We were not, Carolyn said. We were saying how good looking he was. Tell the truth, Jean.

You'll get me hung, Jean said. All right, I admit it. We were talking about more than the playing if I have to be brutally honest.

Good looking, Stephanie said. *And* gifted. You're a very lucky girl.

I expect you know that too, Mona, eh? Carolyn winked.

Oh yes, Mona said. Certainly do.

They laughed this time. Sort of giggled. Mona's glass was needing refilled.

I envy you, though. All that beautiful music going on all the time under your own roof, friendly terms with Wagner and Mendelssohn, the *Moonlight Sonata* raging away next door. Jean sighed. It must be marvellous.

Well. Mona looked at her. He plays mostly contemporary these days. More Maxwell Davies then Mendelssohn. Folk who're still alive kind of thing.

Sorry? Stephanie looked as if she hadn't heard right.

Beamish, Weir, said Mona. Nicholson.

Never mind, said Jean.

What's it like, though, living with that kind of creative talent? Living with it? Carolyn's eyes got bigger. It must be terribly romantic.

Oh you get used to it, Mona said. You . . . um . . . cope.

Maybe Mona is a musician too, though, said Stephanie. Creative people often team up with other creative people, the shared sensitivities and everything. I bet you're a musician too. Am I right?

No, I'm not a musician, Mona said.

She couldn't see Heather any more. Her voice was still there though, the word *sensual* rising and fading back into the continuous buzz from somewhere else.

Shame, Carolyn said. Still it's probably just as well. Somebody needs to be the practical one, able to do the organising and things. She took Mona's glass and put it on a passing tray, served them both another. Sorting out his music and concert clothes and so on.

Did you see his fingers? Jean looked at Stephanie. They're solid! Solid muscle!

Really? Stephanie looked horrified.

They're *huge*. Literally. Bulging. People don't think about it as a physical job do they? But there you are. Literally bulging.

I bet he's impractical though. Carolyn again. Creative people are famous for it. I bet being close to that sort of person has its downside.

Well, Mona said.

Not good with time-keeping I bet.

Well. Mona wasn't sure she should be saying this but she said it anyway. He doesn't dust or anything. I lift a lot of socks up.

It is though isn't it? Jean was fiddling with her hair, drawing her fingers through it, separating the lacquered sheets. Physical, I mean. Does he train?

Mona could hear Danny's voice close enough to whisper to. That's my job, after all, he was saying. That's part of what people pay me to do. Someone must have asked him how he remembered all those notes. A man laughed as though the answer was a joke of some kind and there was the sound of a hand slapping a back.

No, Mona said. He doesn't train. Unless lifting beer-glasses counts.

Jean laughed and shook her head as though Mona was a real wag, a card. Good for you, she said. Haha. Good for you.

They all smiled at each other again. Something had reached a natural conclusion. Mona looked into her orange juice and Stephanie and Carolyn began a slow drift in the direction of the buffet table. Danny's voice, further off but still clean as a triangle, was asking where the toilets were.

Well, Jean said. It's been a pleasure meeting you. She was turning away, not sure how to make the break without feeling she was doing the wrong thing. And that *charming* husband.

Mona smiled, nodded.

And tell him, Jean stage-whispered, that lovely man of yours, tell him he's *wonderful*. Flashing aren't-I-awful eyes before she faded further off. Behind her back, Mona saw Danny heading off out the door. One hand in the pocket, raking for fags. Mona kept smiling till Jean turned away.

The buffet table was crowded now, mostly women: more empty glasses dotted round the place than full ones. Mona thought about going over and couldn't be bothered. Up too early again, bed too late,

Danny haring about with an iron before breakfast. Getting here. You got out of practice for being out: rusty for dealing with people. All they knew was work, when you thought about it: Danny in his room all the time with the bloody piano, crashing away till midnight depending what else he'd had to do that day, her trying to write at the kitchen table till godknows. They hardly knew how to deal socially with each other never mind other people. And then there was the dizziness, the waves of nausea that washed up these days. What she wanted was a lie down. There was a chair over on the far side of the room with no-one near it, just a man looking out the big bay window. The chair looked soft and Danny wouldn't be long. The man looked ok too: preoccupied. Safe. She was just about to go over when something touched her back.

A man was standing behind her with a wee book of some kind. It wasn't a concert programme, just a book.

Sorry, he said. Didn't mean to do that.

He had very pale skin, freckles on his scalp. That's ok, Mona said. Just don't do it again.

It was meant to be funny, light or something but he just looked at her and didn't say anything. His eyes were watery, filmed over. He looked not well.

Sorry, she said.

No, he said. I am. My line.

Right, she said. The watery eyes kept looking at her. Mona gesticulated towards the chair. Just . . . um . . . heading over here then.

What d'you think of this lot? he said. He rustled the booklet between his hands. Lot of money to run an orchestra.

Mona looked at him. Maybe he hadn't heard her. Maybe she hadn't heard him, the wheezy voice needing to be listened to harder to get more of a gist.

People don't think about where it comes from, he said. Money.

The chair was still free. Mona could see it. The man was looking out at the night skyline.

Dependent on things they know nothing about. He wiped his mouth suddenly, the white end of a hanky disappearing back inside the jacket pocket. Parasitic. The whole thing. All parasites.

The feeling in Mona's stomach was intensifying. It told her she wanted to get away but she couldn't think how. How to do it refused to occur.

The people who come to concerts. Ignorant. Like everybody else. Mona waited.

Am I not being interesting enough? he said suddenly.

No, Mona said. She said it without thinking. No you're being. You're being what you're being.

People who come to concerts, he said again. He looked at the floor.

You're not the kind of people who come to concerts, then?

Oh yes, he said. Wife likes them. Women do. His eyes scanned the parquet. I'm also the director-general of this outfit. It's sort of expected.

Something like a wince moved over his mouth, faded out. It was hard to tell whether he didn't know she hadn't a clue what he was talking about or simply didn't care. He kept looking down.

Right, she said.

They stood for a moment saying nothing.

Not a musician yourself, are you? He rolled the sore-looking eyes towards her briefly, lowered them again.

No, she said. You're safe there.

He made the half-smile. No I'm not, he said. You're a sympathiser. I can tell. I know you're thinking I'm a fool. A Philistine.

Oh?

You sense it, he said. Like a smell.

Mona had had enough. She didn't want any more of whatever this was. Not tonight.

It's what's wrong, he said. What's wrong with the whole country.

Mona said nothing.

No servant class.

Mona looked suddenly at him. She couldn't help it. She stood very still, just looking.

Given up our servant class. Self-evident that's no good. You look at the great civilisations and you'll see: give up your servant class and it all goes to hell. Too many people who don't know anything. They're not getting the proper guidance. Not getting a job where they're given reliable instruction. What are they supposed to do?

Mona didn't know.

Express themselves, he said. They go about expressing themselves.

He waved the paper limply, scanned the room. They had stopped looking at each other.

Doesn't build pyramids, does it?

Pyramids, Mona said. She kept watching him, the ironic smile or whatever it was, twitching at the corners of his mouth. Pyramids, she said again. There was nothing else in the room to attach to. Not a thing. The man near the window had moved away and you couldn't even see the streetlights from here. She watched black sky for a while. Then spoke.

My mother was a servant, she said. She was in service for eight years.

So was mine. The shape of him at the corner of her eye not budging. Interesting we should have that in common.

Stephanie was there suddenly, fussing.

Do you want anything Archie? He never eats properly. She raised her eyebrows, the pencil lines moving into mock-furious arches. I need to do everything for him.

She wiped his lapels and took the booklet out of his hand. He just stood there, letting her and Mona saw for the first time what it was. A score. He'd been in at the concert, if he'd been in at all, with a concerto score. Without it to hold into, his hand started shaking. It trembled over the slit of his jacket pocket as though he was trying to pull out a stuck scarf. Like he had Parkinson's or something.

Go away, Stephie, he said. He was doing his smile, shifting the top lip. It occurred to Mona he might have had a stroke. She looked over at Stephanie and Stephanie smiled. Very gently.

Go away, he said again. She went.

Well, Mona said. She could see Danny at the door now, the travel bag over one arm, waving for her to come. Her coat was there too. Well. It's been . . . whatever.

Yes, he said. It has.

He reached to take the empty glass from her. He held onto it when she passed it to him, drew her nearer.

You despise me, don't you? he said.

It was just the same tone of voice he'd used all evening: even, disinterested.

I can see that too.

His eyes looked coated.

I don't know you, she said. She let the glass go. I know nothing about you. Of course I don't despise you.

You know the Koechel number of that concerto? The one they did tonight? The tempo for the second movement?

No, Mona said.

Thought not, he said. Neither does that young man.

I have to go now. She said it quite definitely, quite sure. She wanted away from him: this dying individual with his score tucked under his arm, thinking Mozart had written an instruction manual just for him, a set of tips on form. If she didn't go soon she'd say something and let Danny down. It was his do, not hers. This was Danny's work for godsake, not hers. Goodbye, she said. She walked away without turning round, hoping she had sounded calm. Jean and Carolyn weren't anywhere. Heather was dancing. Only Stephanie waved.

Christ I thought you were never coming, he said when she got out. He was pacing from foot to foot like he was frozen. Come on then. I'm dying for a fish supper.

Mona took Danny's tails on their hanger, her own coat.

You got your flowers? she said.

He hauled the tulips from under the sports bag, hers too. The roses. Mona had almost forgotten about them.

Don't tell me, he said. Simon said they weren't for me.

Mona nodded.

I told him you were pregnant. Did you tell him as well?

Mona looked Danny hard in the eye, put one hand on his shoulder. The cloth of his jacket was warm, grainy.

Danny, she said. Her stomach was tight. What was the Koechel number of the concerto?

Eh? he said. He stopped bouncing.

The K number. D'you know it?

Four-six-six, he said.

Mona looked at him.

Look, you don't spend months with a piece, seeing it every day without knowing the Koechel number. I can give you the date of the first performance as well if you like. Eleventh of February, seventeen-eighty-five. And his dad was there. Not that they've got anything to do with anything but I'm throwing in extra free. What kind of question's that supposed to be? Koechel number?

Danny, she said. She pulled him closer. He smelled of cigarette smoke, aftershave and sweat. A man after his work. Danny, tell me our child will not have to play the piano for a living, Danny. Tell me.

He looked at her hard, his eyebrows tangled up. Mona kept her face dead straight.

Mona, he said quietly. I haven't a clue what you're talking about. Not a clue.

I know, she said. Are you going to tell me anyway?

No, he said. Of course I'm not.

She knew that too.

Can I assume the daft questions concluded? He smiled when he said it but he was getting fed up with this, whatever it was. He wanted his chips and he wanted them now. Mona said nothing. Danny flexed his hands. Come on, Mona. It's perishing in here.

He stopped for the plastic carrier, the straps of the overnight bag. The blond trumpet-player came out the reception room rubbing his temples.

Thank god that's over, he said. He nodded in their direction. See you in the pub ok?

He walked off, shaking his head, down the corridor after his case.

Mona watched him. When she turned back, Danny was standing, the weight of the big bag digging a groove into his shoulder. He was fit for the road.

Ok? The take-away on the corner. We'll catch the pubs as well if you're quick. He smiled like the sun coming out, kissed her cheek and started walking.

Mona watched Danny moving towards the night air outside, his flowers under one arm. Her wrist was sore, the hanger with the tails biting into her fingers. It was so bloody heavy. She looked down at the thing, the stubborn crimson lining, hearing the sound of his footfalls recede. Monkey-jackets they called them. Livery. Faint laughter was drifting from behind the closed door. Danny walked on ahead, two bunches of flower-heads bobbing under his arm. She hadn't even told him how good he'd been, how proud she was of him. His work. And that, she realised suddenly, was what she very much wanted to say. Yellow tulips still fresh beneath the artificial light.

I love you, Danny.

It was exactly what she wanted to say.

a night in

The door gave on the third shove. Stevie said it hadn't even hurt his shoulder.

There were workmen's things dotted about over the floor, boards rolling with strings of stour the size of carpet bales. We had seen the bales from outside, the shapes of them showing through the scaffolding by the light they hung on the gables overnight and hoped they might be insulating stuff, something we could use for covers. Just dust, though, fluff and unplaceable debris. Stevie kicked the nearest and it scudded away like a fish scouring the bottom of a tank. Like something living. Near to, the planks were plaided with squares of brightness from the security light outside, regular shapes crayoned thick blue. Their footprints became apparent as we walked: tyre-prints from the rims of work-shoes, a freestanding cast of someone's sole in mud, deep enough to hold water. We found an empty beer can, cigarette cartons, rags of newspaper. Nothing else. The lamp with the cable, a wire grid over the bulb, might have been a warm thing but we couldn't get it to work. Even if we had managed, it would have been too risky, drawn the attention of foremen or other people doing rounds, neighbourhood watch people maybe, checking. At least with the light not on we'd be all right for a wee bit longer. Cold maybe. But dry. Stevie put the thing down when he realised and stood up, fished in his inside pocket. He did one of those slow smiles at me. I could hear it, even in the dark, the sound of some kind of pleasure buttering his face before he lit them, three single matches one after the other. They all blew out. There was no glass in the windows yet, just open holes. Holes in every wall. He held up the fourth match to the ceiling to get it out of the draught so it stayed lit. I saw two shadows dart the length of the boards from under our feet and, on either side, the skeleton of the building flaring, flickering up like flame. The vertiginous height of scaffolding, the weight of this structure that hung over our heads.

The first time I'd seen anything like that, what keeps a house standing. I remember thinking how special it was. A privilege. We were seeing something intimate, something the people whose home this would become would never see or even think about. Cats had walked through here, bedded down in the dust where they felt safe. Birds maybe, insects would have pitted into the unplastered brick. And us. They would never know about us, what had passed through here before their occupation: the way it had looked rolling with ersatz tumbleweed, the windows gaping like torn posters off motorway hoardings. The wind flapped the plastic sheeting, the scaffolding whining like someone asleep, wrestling with dreams and I knew it for sure, for dead certain sure. We had been here and they would never have a bloody clue.

At least I wasn't alone. I tried to remember that when the match died, leaving everything darker than before. I wasn't alone so it wasn't frightening. We both stayed still, maybe thinking the same thing, till the filter of light from the safety lamp outside started to make a difference again. I remember seeing the shapes of my feet inside the wet shoes, flexing my toes to make them feel more real. The space opening out beside me that was Stevie moving away and whistling. I watched him walk across the boards, the back of his coat glittering with sunk-in rain. It'll do he said, squatting down in one corner: It'll do. And he opened out his coat. He held open his coat till I came towards him, letting me know it was all right. I looked at him, the dark patches where his eyes would be, trying not to shiver, looking into the still space inside the house that gave nothing away. And he started singing. Not words, not the kind of tune you could recognise, but singing anyway. That's what he was doing when the lightning came. I was walking towards him and he was singing, opening out his coat for me to come when the flash lit everything up with sore white light. Rain from nowhere heavy as running on the roof and the single snapshot of this place that would be a room, Stevie in one of its corners, waiting for me. He pulled me tight towards him then, folding me up inside the damp material. And we looked together out of the window space, the place that would be shut up with glass, waiting for thunder.

test

Rustling.

Shoes through dry leaves. Through crisp pokes.

There was someone in the room.

Large hands were uncovering something from inside brown paper,
carefully. There was someone moving around in here, thinking her
unconscious. Lying prone in the halfdark, Mhairi stiffened. The too-
close wall was making goosepimples along her arm, her nerves
bristling. Like her skin was contracting, trying to make less of itself.
Under the covers, the tee-shirt was rucked to her waist. She was half-
asleep, belly-naked. Prone. The sound came again, tickling the hair on
the back of her neck. The crackle of someone unwrapping a claw
hammer. A length of cable.
Cheesewire.

Mhairi held the same inbreath in her lungs, waiting, till her ribs
started to hurt. Nothing happened. She waited some more, listening.
There was nothing to hear but her own heartbeat, the slow whisper of
air down her nostrils as she metered the outbreath it wasn't possible to
keep back. HELLO? she said. Her eyelashes were separating.
HELLO? Whatever it was, she wanted to meet it on good terms. And
her eyes were open.

Curtained halfdark. The air looked grainy, full of hidden spaces. She ran her eyes over surfaces, into corners: the side of the washhand basin, the blur of telly, the daft ceramic nativity set she'd insisted on hauling all the way south, its hardly-any-watt bulb still on. Green figures on the dresser blinking 7.15 7.15 7.15 were the only thing moving. Nothing else. Nothing discernible anyway. She sat up, checking, trying not to feel the curdled something-or-other slopping like brandy in her stomach. Her bra was digging in, underwires biting the top of her ribcage. But she wasn't for taking it off. Those shooting pains when she tried to do without the damn thing, even for a couple of hours, were worse. Like a heart-attack gone wrong. The big girl's burden, Patrick called it. Haha Patrick haha. It was sore though. Her head too, thumping like a radio in another room. There was paracetamol somewhere but godknew. Mhairi imagined getting up and looking for it, putting the wee chalk circles in her mouth, that taste like bile writhing. The stink of bacon didn't help. Bacon, sausages, toast done on one side and eggs. The kitchen right under her room: you could smell burnt pig fat if you put your nose too close to the wallpaper. Mhairi thought about Mrs Easter down somewhere under her floorboards, frying eggs: mucous coatings over pale yolks, bubbles in the whites. Like diseased crocodile eyes. Christ almighty. At least there was no axe-murderer as well. There was no sound at all. No coughs or running water, no belt buckles clanking; that quietness of razors against stubble that meant the men in the next room were still around. Nothing. Godknew what time they started on building sites, why the guys who worked over the road stayed here. Being away did that: it made you realise there were a million things about how the world was ordered, tiny, necessary things about life you knew damn all about. Things your grandfather never told you. He'd given her the nativity set, though. Just Mary and two wise men, a shepherd and a sheep but it had been complete once. Melchior had got stood on, the crib was empty and godknew where Joseph was. But it made her feel safer or something. Mhairi looked at it, smiled. And smelled the bacon again. She turned away, swallowed hard a couple of times. There was nothing for it. She'd have to put on the telly.

Mhairi stretched, pressed the button with her foot. White almonds reared out of the screen and turned into three tortoises chasing a rat. Cartoons. Mhairi didn't like cartoons. Even as a wee girl she hadn't liked them, except Dumbo. She couldn't remember who'd taken her to see it. It wouldn't have been grandad. But she remembered the film fine. The thought of Dumbo reaching for the big elephant's trunk through the bars of a cage could still make her eyes water. Not the stuff they put on these days though. Godknew what they were meant to be about, what weans saw in them. She let the turtles run for another minute anyway. Then a man and a woman came on, pretending to be chummy over cups of coffee. After the news, they said, have WE got something for YOU: the men who've been skinny-dipping in the Serpentine since January the first, the woman who's just given birth at the age of fifty-five and a new hard-hitting report that claims more children are likely to turn to suicide at this time of year than at any other. The man lurched forward out of his comfy chair, looking hard at Mhairi. Join us after the news when our phone lines will be waiting for your Festive Fallout Heartbreak call. Mhairi turned to sort out the pillow while he said the number and the news tune played. When she turned back, the eyes were there. Those big eyes that only very young children have. There was another fucking crisis in Bosnia. Little girls with scarves over their mouths in the snow, dusty white feet poking out of stained carpet coffins, women greeting. There were always women greeting. You couldn't hear them because the report was dubbed over the top of the film but you could see them all right. There would be a full report later. After that, a missing toddler found buried in an open field, a woman raped by a SAFE HOME AT NIGHT taxi driver, a drug-ring in Staffordshire and Tiger the dog. Tiger had been saved from a disused well shaft with only minor cuts and grazes. Tiger was ok. Mhairi turned the sound down and went over to the wash-stand.

The tube was flat. Sucked dry. Mhairi forced what was left inside onto the brush and threw the wasted container in the bin under the sink and something crackled. Something familiar. Slowly, she looked down. Under the individual milk tubs, paled-out tea-bags, kirbies, tissues, clumps of shed hair, the sandwich containers. Clear moulded plastic with the sticky label still intact. She reached forward, the brush angled in her mouth, touched the empty triangles with one finger. They crackled. Twice. Then again without her touching this time. The burglar/rapist/nameless intruder. It was a sandwich tray. The thing she'd said HELLO to, hoping politeness would make it less inclined to do real damage. HELLO for godsake. It was a sandwich tray. Mhairi straightened, brushing her teeth hard, acknowledging her own eyes in the mirror. Another grey hair right in the middle of the fringe. She pulled it out, spat, rinsed, shaking her head. HELLO for godsake. On the way past to the wardrobe, the folded jeans, she switched off the holiday commercials playing steel guitar to the empty bed and opened the wardrobe.

It wasn't cold and the men from the site didn't yell. Mhairi walked with her head up. A girl, maybe fourteen or fifteen, with no jacket and crutches was there just beyond the grass verge, hovering on the kerb for the sign to change. She could see her quite clearly: the first carefully placed step onto the road and the car coming round the curve of the park. The car accelerating. The lights had to be against him but he didn't seem to be slowing down any, just keeping coming. Mhairi was wondering if she should shout when the girl stopped. She stopped on the crossing with her arms at her sides and watched the thing coming towards her. Mhairi stopped too. At the last minute, the car swerved, brakes squealing at the white line. The tyres bumped the pavement as it stopped. And the girl was fine. Still there, absolutely fine. Mhairi watched the driver's window roll down, the man in the passenger seat turn away while his pal started roaring. The girl swivelled on the crutches and walked on, step for step, to the other side. As if she couldn't hear.

Stupid bitch, he yelled.

Nothing.

You could've caused a bloody accident.

From the other side, she turned back briefly. Prick, she said. Then walked on under the trees. By the time Mhairi reached the crossing the guy was back in his seat, combing his hair. Stupid bitch, he said again, loud enough for Mhairi to hear. Then drove off. He left behind a fresh skid-line, back rubber tread against the grey asphalt. There was no-one else on the whole stretch of road. Mhairi ignored three green men and checked the road umpteen times. Just in case.

The park wasn't really. Only a few hankies of grass, a dozen trees with warty-looking branches. It took no more than two minutes to walk through going slow. She could see the mall sign now, star-shaped fairy-lights still showing between the bare branches, SALE notices shouldering into view beneath. This morning there were buds as well. Tight, unidentifiable, but definitely buds, the sky behind them the colour of a medical card. She'd liked this walk from the first day: five minutes across the green and two sets of lights, then down the pedestrian area to the gallery. She didn't need to be there at all now. Her stuff was all set up and Debbie did the selling but she liked to call in every day, rearrange the brooches a bit, hang around and talk. Watching folk try on the things she'd made was good, having folk know who you were when you walked in somewhere. Like you belonged. Even not meaning to go till later, this was the way she was walking. Besides, the best shops were near the gallery, Patrick and Maureen's presents still to go. Maureen was easy: she liked anything that was ear-rings. One of the other silverworkers in the exhibition had promised her a pair in exchange for a pair of Mhairi's. Patrick was harder. Tapes were always the wrong band or the subject of HOW COULD ANYBODY LIKE THAT CRAP monologues and clothes were too dear. Anyway, she'd look. Then buy him beer. It was a pig to carry back but you couldn't go wrong with Patrick and beer. Then grandad. Didn't drink, didn't smoke, didn't read or use aftershave, didn't play cards, dominoes or football. He didn't play anything. Christ, Patrick had said the first time she told him about him, he sounds like a right miserable old bastard; is he the Pope? and Mhairi had smiled but not properly, not meaning it. She was thinking. She was wondering, mibby for the first time, what other people thought. If it was the way she was talking about him or if he really was a miserable old bastard. He made his garden sculptures and drove his taxi, went to the spiritualist church and tried to send messages to Mhairi's ma and grandma. That was what he did. Sum total. Since he'd packed in the fishing boats, he'd more or less stayed at home all the time. He didn't even watch tv. Anyway, it made him hell to buy presents for. The worst was the Christmas she'd given him tarot cards and he'd chucked them in the fire. Mistake. Keeping it simple was safest. Socks. He had drawers full of socks, the bands still on. It would be nice to get him something he'd really like but godknew what it was. More and more, especially now she'd moved away, he acted like presents were a waste of money. Something he wouldn't thank you for. As though you were a fool for trying to get him something nice. Mibby Patrick was right.

The shops were there now, the rest of the arcade stretching down the hill, rack outside Jezebel and sale labels visible all the way up the street. JEZEBEL in dayglo green, dripping, and underneath, her shoes. Cuban heel, suede, scarlet. She walked by them every day, imagining Maureen looking at them, talking to her as though she was off her head: they're dear, they're a funny colour, they're hopeless material, get something *practical*, Mhairi. Maureen was keen on *practical*: there was never any arguing about what it was and those shoes weren't. Patrick would be more succinct. He'd tell her they looked like something a tart would wear/had she paid for them/they must have seen her coming. That said, though, he'd like them fine. Grandad wouldn't even see them. He'd never been to Glasgow for ages. These days there were lots of things he didn't know. The fact her hair was a different colour for one thing. And short. And Patrick, that she and Patrick weren't just in the same house any more, they were in the same room. The same bed. He was funny enough about Patrick's existing near her never mind anything else. Mhairi stood still for a long moment, looking down the slope at the shoe racks, imagining the feel of suede under her hand. Wicked, gorgeous, wonderful. And not really for her. They were all quite right. She didn't need them. Nobody did, she supposed. A wave of nausea washed at the back of her throat. What she really needed wasn't shoes, it was indigestion tablets. There was a decent cafe just over the road, the door open and waiting. What she really needed right now was a sit down.

Five servings of milk. She slipped them into her pocket out of eyeshot of the woman serving along with four sugar sachets and a couple of teaspoons for good measure, then sat down at the window with the hot cup. Other wee odds and sods were still in the bag from yesterday but it paid to think ahead. Mrs Easter never gave her enough for the amount of tea she was drinking down here. And postcards. The postcards were still in there as well, not written yet. There was nothing to put because they phoned all the time. Every night so she didn't have to go out alone to a callbox, making sure she was keeping herself safe. Trying to tell them things that made it worth their bother wasn't so easy. It was hard to say what it was like at all, the difference being away.

They didn't know the people she'd met, what the names meant when she used them. Maureen always laughed in the right places but Maureen did that. Even if she didn't know what the hell you were talking about. She always laughed in the wrong bits. It made Mhairi feel awkward and embarrassed, as if she was talking another language badly. Describing the New Year thing with Debbie and Frankie, going out for a meal, staying on in the restaurant with five Algerian waiters behind the locked door, drinking godknew what to bring in the bells and singing Pavarotti hits in different languages and kid-on Italian. Total strangers. Debbie with the purple hair who made necklaces out of shells. Frankie wearing Lycra shorts and a rubber swimming hat with roses round the ears. When it came to it, though, Mhairi couldn't remember why it had been so good, couldn't tell it right at all. Patrick was the worst. He'd listened till she stopped then there was a silence on his side of the phone.

So what did you eat then? he said eventually.

Something with lentils, Mhairi said.

Oh? he said.

Egyptian Pie.

Oh?

Debbie said they called it that because it tasted like sand.

Should have had an omelette, then.

Yes, she said.

She knew Patrick was waiting for her to say something more but she couldn't think of anything. They'd done his gig in Edinburgh, Maureen's night in with her mum. She couldn't think of anything else.

So, he said. You had a good time?

Yes. She felt apologetic saying it. Yes.

Great. A long pause. You had a good time.

Maybe he'd hoped she'd need more encouragement or something, more reassurance she was fine elsewhere. Maybe he got a shock hearing her not needing it. And it *was* shocking somehow. How fine she felt. How perfectly all right. And she had missed him then, in the callbox near the bus shelter where the same two drunks hung about every afternoon asking for money: the hiss that might have been some form of loneliness coming down the wire. On the other hand, mibby that was just sentimental nonsense. Patrick always said she read too much into things, exaggerated what he said to suit herself. As though he thought she was trying to trap him, make him admit more than he felt. Maybe she was. Anyway she didn't want to start hiding things. She'd tell him about the evening the gallery staff had planned for her last day and hope he'd be pleased. Four days more. Then she'd be back, Glasgow Central by half eight. He'd be out with the band and not able to meet the train but he'd want to know. He usually liked to know. That was what she could put on the postcard, then. She put the cards next to the saucer, foraged in her bag for a pen. It came out with pink mush all over the tip. Lipstick. The top off the bloody thing again. The card she'd been saving for Patrick was wearing it too – a sheeny pink blob over the bit where his name would be. Imagining his face, lifting it from behind the door. He'd think she'd kissed the damn thing before she'd posted it and think she'd gone off her head. She dabbed the mark one more time, laughing, knowing it wouldn't shift.

The chemist was next to the post box. By the afternoon, there were queues at all the tills but right now was fine. Two walls of tissues, floor to head-height. Different colours or sizes, for make-up and sneezing into, pocket-size, travel-size, man-size, menthol, baby-soft: umpteen ply and pastels, Noddies, Postman Pats. Two walls. Mhairi took the cheapest and looked round for the sandwiches. They were visible from here but she didn't want to walk over. Not yet. Thinking about fillings was making her feel sick. She held the edge of the nearest counter and waited for it to subside, sweating. The caffeine, maybe. These places were always too hot. Another wave reminding her how much alcohol she'd drunk last night. There was a seat near the prescription counter, there behind the cotton wool and sterilising fluid. She knew exactly where it was. Behind the pink and blue boxes. Mhairi flicked her eyes in their direction, not sure why it mattered not to be seen. She'd spent half an hour there yesterday, gone out without buying. This time, the dizziness was more pressing. She walked over, sat on her heels holding the nearest shelf. It was daft to feel embarrassed. But the prices. Jesus. What was there in a Pregnancy Testing Kit that justified that kind of money – more than half the price of the too-dear shoes? She looked at the side, the words in clean white lettering.

> Contents: two phials of testing solution (with lids),
> two colour tablets, two indicator wands, dropper, instruction sheet.
> ACCURATE FROM THE FIRST DAY OF THE MISSED PERIOD.

The clinic said to wait another three weeks when she phoned, they'd have preferred six. Mhairi thought she hadn't heard right, the accent or maybe a bad line. But it was right enough. Six weeks. She told them she wasn't here that long and they said it wasn't their problem. She hung up. Now here was this box, telling her she could know now. Tomorrow morning. Before she went home and had to look at Patrick, work out how to be. She looked at the package, the price flash on the shelf. A purple anorak sleeve reached over her head. It took something from the shelf, retracted. The woman who owned it, a girl maybe, was standing behind her, reading one of the boxes. No make-up and her hair pulled back like that. She looked about seventeen.

Doesn't matter which one you lift, does it? she said. They're all complicated.

Mhairi smiled. Expensive as well.

Sorry?

54

Mhairi felt noticeable suddenly, shy. They're dear, I'm saying. Pricey.

The woman laughed. You think we could wait. Not as though you don't know soon enough eh?

She put the box back into the rack and walked away, bumping the wire basket off her thigh. It was full of babyfood. She walked back to the checkout carrying it, collecting a pushchair to wheel it through, a huge infant in a snowsuit plumped up like an inflatable doll inside it. Its wee eyes peered out, not blinking. Mhairi hadn't a clue how old it might be, had no way of even guessing. Its mother maybe expecting again, half Mhairi's age by the looks of her, and here was Mhairi with no information on certain vital subjects at all. Vital female subjects. She looked down. Boy-blue cardboard, tidy graphics: a clock with a quarter of its face shaded off, a hand holding a phial. It wasn't just the money. The jewellery had gone well. She had sold stuff here, more than she would have at home. There ought to be enough for one-off extravagances. It wasn't just money at all. It was the thought of having to pee straight into a tiny glass container early in the morning, measuring out with the dropper then the waiting, lying back on Mrs Easter's green candlewick, trying not to look at the LED numbers not changing, trying not to think about what this might only be the beginning of, how many more samples and testing could come next. Then taking out the indicator. Taking out the indicator. It was still too hot in here. And the black aftertaste in her mouth. Whether she felt this way from her suspicion of what might be true or. Or what. It was hard even to imagine the word. Pregnant. Suddenly the girl-woman was back, reaching for the box she had put back earlier. She looked at Mhairi and shrugged.

Well. She shrugged again, looking caught out. You do, don't you? Her sneakers squeaked as she walked away.

Mhairi looked at the package in her hand. She stood up, carefully.

One knee cricked, needing oiled. The things inside the box shifted with her as she limped towards the till.

Outside was better. Still not wonderful, but fresher. Mhairi stood at the postbox, the polythene bag over her arm, catching her breath. To look busy, she fished the cards out of her bag, pushed them through the slit. She imagined Maureen and Patrick picking them up, knowing whose writing it was. Comparing notes. Four days. She would be back in four days. The presents would have to wait though. The thumping in her head was starting again, a heartbeat in the wrong place. There were benches near the phone kiosk, just a block further up. At the other side of the park. She imagined herself walking into the kiosk, pressing her forehead against the cool metal walls, her finger pressing all the right buttons. Then. Then nothing. It was the wrong time of day. Patrick was never in on Wednesday mornings. He always stayed out after he'd signed on. Maureen was at work. There was no-one to speak to. Except grandad. There was an offchance there. Grandad. She walked till dizziness threatened to make her fall then knelt where she was, the bag at her feet. Breathing out and in slowly, counting. She could see the phone ringing in the wee hall with the brown wallpaper, the holy pictures still there with ancient bits of tinsel left over from Christmas if he'd put any up this year at all, the shore and the electricity pylons visible from the tiny wee window. Barra shut for Wednesday and the phone ringing out. Caitlin Sinclair pushing a pram with the bairn in it she'd been too feart to admit to till she was in labour. Dear god dear god. She couldn't phone him. Not with this terrible danger inside her, the nearness of doing something stupid and she didn't want to do anything stupid. Not before she knew for sure. The best thing to do was wait. Wait, go back for a lie down, and everything would be fine. She'd hear them tonight: Patrick would phone and Maureen would phone and she would listen to them in Mrs

Easter's kitchen, trying not to notice the smell of dead meat laid out for the morning, their voices not knowing yet, not treating her any different. And later, even when they did, if they did, she'd still be fine. Fine. She might have to be finer than she'd ever been in her life. For now, though, there were simple practicalities. The cafe, the road and the park one step at a time. Mhairi looked up, gauging the distance. A face caught her off-guard, a face staring at her from the window of the shoe shop across the road. Her own. Just a glass reflection. If you refocused, employed a simple trick of the eye, it went away. All you could see were red shoes. She watched them for a moment then looked back down the mall. All that way to the chemist's and she'd forgotten the toothpaste. She sighed, sniffed, lifted her bags. Back at Mrs Easter's she'd make a list.

TOOTHPASTE, SANDWICHES, BEER, EAR-RINGS, SOCKS wrote itself in her head as she walked under the trees: a neat row in red biro, the handwriting she won gold stars for. At the other side of the park, the word WOOL appeared. WOOL. They said her grandad had used to knit, all the fishermen had. They'd wound oily wool round their big, gristly fingers, been self-sufficient, made their own jerseys. To hell with socks. She'd get him wool, take it herself and watch his face when he opened it; the surprise before he'd had time to control it. At least it would be some kind of reaction. Mhairi laughed till it started to turn into something else then stopped. Wool. His hands the way they were. He couldn't knit now even if he wanted to. If he ever had. She wasn't going to greet though. Greeting made you dangerous. It made you sentimental and that was no bloody use to anybody. Whatever happened, she wasn't going to give in. She wasn't going back to Barra, she wasn't greeting and she wasn't giving in. She had to remember that. She'd survive. People did. They had the capacity to survive. Another thing. She was going back for another look at those shoes. This afternoon, before some other bugger bought them. She'd write that down as well.

The trees were thinning out and the main road was visible. Someone whistled, shouted over from the building site. Mhairi heard but didn't look round. Prick, she said under her breath. Prick. Black tyre skids snaked under her feet as she walked over the crossing with her head up, breathing deep for a lungful of fresh air. It wasn't fresh at all, it was full of carbon monoxide. But it was fine. It would do. Dear god but she wanted to hear his voice. Walking, glass phials chiming at her heels, the sky blue as burning.

after the rains

think

it is too warm here and my heart is racing think where was I I was

in the bus shelter.

Dripping in there with the rest of them out of the rain.

It must have been shortly after ten because the bus to the Cross had just drawn up, the brakes still squealing and when they stopped there was a sound of nothing. That was what was different. I remember distinctly, the silence. The sound of people listening to each other listening. We peered, curled pieces of ourselves beyond the perspex, testing from under rain-mates for what it was. I watched an elder bush, the nearest of the seven planted by the council to represent nature on the estate. Its leaves dripped still. But I could swear the drops were less assured now, visible seconds lurching between one drop and the next as I watched. A child standing near me ducked and looked up, suddenly suspicious. With a muffled grunt that could have been apology, a large woman shoved by me and out into the middle of the road to make sure for all of us. We watched her stand there, face upturned. The slow, steady smile. In that moment, we knew. It had stopped raining. After nine solid months, it had stopped raining. Folk normally so wary, so shy of ridicule it hurt, we blossomed. We cracked jokes and spoke to perfect strangers, we embraced

like warm soup to remember it, the touch of human skin

while the bus sat like a ruin on the road. There was laughing and cuddling and general pagan revelry. Some of the passengers got off the bus and joined us as we emerged from the shelter, one shaking a bottle of lemonade with his thumb over the neck, spraying it like champagne. The driver was out too. Even given the mood that was remarkable since he was usually such a bloodyminded big bastard. He looked, he saw, he made a hammy mime of looking at his watch. Right, he said. The rain was off. We'd seen what there was to see. If anybody's goin to the Cross they better come wi me, he said. Some of us have got schedules to keep. Nobody minded. We came, good-natured to spite him: we drifted back. Then, as I straggled on, I noticed something in the corner of the shelter: a wee girl, huddling in on herself, keeking out between her fingers. I watched her as the bus began to move, indistinct behind too much hair. Something in my stomach fluttered but that was all. Maybe I should have been more curious, taken time. The bus picked up speed, though. With the rest I let myself be taken and my excitement eclipsed her.

The road itself was interesting now the rain had stopped. Commonplaces became significant as we noted with genuine feeling it was 'turning out nice' or 'taking a turn for the better'. Puddles in the gutters seemed just as full but elsewhere, tarmac was surfacing. You could see boys on the crest of the road, in the middle of the traffic path, for the novelty of standing there without water tugging at their shoes. As we entered the town, a gang of youths were kicking planks away. Everyone hated the planks. Stretched kerb to kerb by selfish old people too afraid of the road tides to attempt crossing without them, they caused accidents, cost limbs, the lives of children. It was like a blessing, a sign of something better to come to see those boys kicking the planks away. Someone sang a hymn. The rest of us pointed and waved, rubbing with cuffs at the windows streaming with our too-close breath, the damp smoking from our clothes. Talk seemed abnormally loud: it wasn't just that we had more to say, but that the noise of drizzle no longer deadened everything. Too much for some, maybe. Too soon. A few near me were in tears and a low groaning could be heard from the upper deck. I thought it had nothing to do with me. I thought it would pass. When the bus stopped at the terminus, I left without giving it further thought.

Only half an hour later, the sky had lightened considerably. Offices and shop windows were framed with workers looking out. I could see rows of them from my bench at the corner of the pedestrian precinct. I was

what was I doing?
just looking too looking up I was

looking up when suddenly, without warning, the sun came out. A great rip in the cloud and there it was: one whole, flaming presence. And with it came the colours. Colours. With a catch of emotion, I realised how much we had forgotten, how ashen everything had been for so long. The low light, the constant smurr – we had encouraged it. For some children, greyness was all there ever had been, was all we were entitled to. Now everything returned, yellows, greens, reds, oranges and wild blues shaming in their brightness. From all over the Cross came a sigh of relief and wonder. We realised how little we had fought. Yet the sun had come out. The sun had come out.

Those of us in the street found the windows of the television showrooms: we were, after all, only ordinary folk and untrusting of the evidence of our own eyes. For a moment or two, there was only a cookery demonstration, a chopping of knives. Then the first news flash. Words typed themselves over sliced vegetables as we watched. Letter by letter it spelled out what we had hoped. The sun had come out. Reassured, as though we knew it all along, we cheered. Laughter died away as a blender mushed solid matter to a pulp behind the printout. A huge pair of hands pulled the top off the glass canister, spilling its dark contents into a bowl before the food disappeared altogether and a man appeared, keen to explain with radiating lines and velcro symbols about the weather. He did that for five minutes, then read cheerfully from a slip of paper. Scientists were confident this was the end of the rain for some considerable time, he said. There would be a full report later and news flashes throughout the day. The Queen was preparing a statement. A picture of her shaking hands with the Prime Minister flickered over the monitor briefly. Both were smiling. Satisfied, we turned away from the tv and shone our faces upwards, crunching our eyes against the unaccustomed sky. I remember my scalp tingling, the back of my neck rippling with a warmth. On all sides, shop workers clustered in open doorways, filled their display windows with faces tilting towards the light. As if it had been waiting for this moment, a massive, seven-coloured arch appeared, pouring itself above the buildings and the town to prickle ready tears. We applauded. We applauded the rainbow and its promise. We were radiant.

By the afternoon it was hot. I hadn't moved much: the length of the street, a little shopping, then back to the bench at the Cross to watch the day unfold along with others who had the time. The streets were misty and dry patches had squared out on the paving. We remarked on the speed of the change of events, but not overmuch. It was enough it was happening at all. City bakeries sold out of sandwiches as people lunched al fresco. Bright dots of tee-shirts began to appear among the crowds. Sloughing off rain-clothes allowed us to look at ourselves afresh and become dissatisfied with what we saw. Those who lived close enough went home to change: canvas trousers, summer dresses, short-sleeved shirts with bleachy angles poking out. Some improvised, rolling up trouser legs in a jokey but serviceable imitation of Bermuda shorts, fit for the tropic the Cross had become. Almost everyone wore a hat, sunglasses or visor against the glare. More news flashes confirmed it: the country was in the grip of a freak heatwave. Temperatures were rising by the minute. The huge plastic thermometer in the travel agent's window bled steadily upward as we rolled up our sleeves and loosened collar-buttons. I went to the riverside walkway seeking cooler air.

cooler there
did I fall asleep? I must have slept
I slept and woke and

By late afternoon, the Cross was much less crowded. Many had drifted off out of the punishing light and gone back indoors to work. Novelty was passing. The crowd under the shade of the Co-op canopy were silent, merely waiting for the bus home. The newsagent's on the corner was shutting, the women who worked there clashing security mesh in place, jangling keys into the stillness. As they crossed the tarmac to the shelter, something pale and smoky billowed out from under their slow-moving soles. It took me a minute to work out it wasn't smoke at all. It was dust. Dust rising up from gutters that had churned with running water for so long. My head thumped. The heat and windlessness of the street was surely intensifying. Workers who had poked their heads from windows earlier to feel the sun on their faces had long since retreated. I couldn't help thinking of them in there

– all that glass. A solitary blind cord tapped listlessly against an overhead pane. Just then the plump woman who owned the flower shop appeared at her open door, wheezing and gasping, the effort of her lungs making her very red about the face and chest in her short summer frock. The OPEN sign swung behind her as she fought for space among the carnations and dahlias. Some other shops were near closing now there was no-one to buy and a few individuals were lowering shutters, keen, I supposed, to get out of the thickening air. The bus queue swelled, sweating. The absence of the hiss of rain had left a vacuum. Cars had quit long since and there was no thrum of flies. It was sickly quiet. Seething. Something

something

was coming. A stretching sound, like a mass intake of breath over our heads was its announcement. Then a low rumble along the horizon, hollowing the ear: distant thunder like men clearing their throats. Ready. It was ready to begin. There was an earth-rippling crack and I looked up. The rainbow was growing, inflating to fill up every stretch of blue till none remained as a touchstone for the sky. At the same time, a huge rushing sound spreading from ear to ear as though some invisible hand were unzipping the hair from my skull. I threw up my hands for protection, seeing others doing the same, some falling on their knees. *Too late for that* . . . There were children too, the odd one or two dancing on the pedestrian walk-way while others were running or clapping their hands. *We are not all seeing the same thing,* I thought, *we are all of us experiencing something far outside the normal run, but,* and the thought horrified me in its obviousness, *but not the same thing.* A glance confirmed it: the faces around me, behind the glass, in doorways and on the road varied extremely. There was barely time to digest the idea when the sound, a terrible sound of high sudden screaming took all attention for itself. Heads turned to find its source.

There, still struggling in her own front doorway, was the florist. She appeared to be trying to pull a shoot *no*

several green shoots she appeared to be trying to pull

several green shoots and leaves from her dress as we watched. More and yet more leaves burst out despite her efforts, and I realised suddenly they were not attached to her dress. They were attached to her elbow, to her arm. I looked harder. They were her arm. *They were her arm.* Greenery surged up her neck and into her hair, buds clustering in a pink halo all around her head. Huge roses ripened at her armpits and elbows; camellias and magnolias fanned out of her cleavage. Seconds or whole minutes, I could not say how long it took. When chrysanthemum petals began falling from somewhere beneath her skirt, the woman stopped struggling. Enough of her face remained however to let me see she was smiling. She was, I realised, welcoming the garden she had become. I felt a twinge of outrage, but as I looked again at the woman's smile and her pleasure, I was moved with compassion. I had to admire it too. The scent was overpowering. It carried all the way from the other side of the road.

In the commotion, we had not noticed a lesser transformation. Her assistant, formerly a girl of about seventeen, now a living display of hyacinth and spring ferns, stepped out from behind the older woman's shadow. At the next doorway, the grocer watched a cabbage foresting the front of his overall. He saw me gaping, hesitated, then pointed at it shyly with his ladyfingers, ears coiling with pea tendrils. The reaction of the crowd to his bravado was enthusiastic. Some cheered and one elderly woman shuffled over for a closer look, muttering endearments. From the back of the bus crowd, a check-out boy I recognised from Tesco's pushed forward to give himself room. The pregnant bulge at the front of his coat was elongating as he came, squaring out to make a trolley complete with front wheel to balance the projection from his body and toddler straps. He did not smile but lowered his shopping into it with great dignity. At the same time, the electrical goods manager of the Co-op displayed a shiny transparent door in the centre of his chest, eager for us to see the bright whorls of washing tumbling inside and receive congratulations on his achievement. All the while the sun grew hotter.

it is too warm here

My arms still cautiously hugging my head, I walked the length of the street to find some shade where I could more comfortably continue to observe. I thought I could see a pattern and wanted to watch it unfold. Though some might have longer gestation periods than others, the transformations would keep going. Loud snickering and the dull rustle of used notes emitted from the bookies as I went past: a squashy bundle emerged from the wool shop. Before long, it would be unstoppable. A whisper was mouthing in my head, half-formed. Perhaps I remembered the child in the shelter from the morning. Something like realisation prickled its beginnings up the back of my neck. I recalled the moaning I had heard on the bus, partial glimpses of things I had chosen to ignore. Without knowing why, I panicked. I ran round the corner, maybe in the hope of escaping, but something blocked my path. An enormous white grub spread the length of the pavement, bulbous tips waving in what looked horribly like appeal. Beyond this nerveless thing, a three-headed phantom groped forward on its hands and knees. Where features should have been was only tight, smooth skin, blanket-grey and eyeless. As another of its kind fumbled from the council offices, nail-less hands foraging for something to give it a sense of its bearings, I drew back, repulsed, fearing the thing it might touch would be me. In so doing, my back touched the wall of the Job Centre, rebounded again at the ripping cold of its walls against my shirt. Even in this heat, frost had feathered the windows and a faint haar issued from the open doorway. I knew nothing would come out of there. Then I was sure. There would be others like this too. Not flowers, not harmless eccentricities, but other things, terrible other things. At that moment, a pitiful screeching forced me to turn. I was facing the butchers'. The howling and the bloody trail at their doorway. The awful death stench and low weeping of children, childish voices seeping under the door of the church.

I would not look in there
I did not want to see

I began to run then. Faster. Curiosity pushed my glance down despite the urgings of reason. My hands were very pale and whitening still. Thinning.

They were stark white.

I kept on running.

waiting for marilyn

Rita's

Rita's

Rita's flashes backwards behind the net.

Multicoloured plastic strips shield a cavity in the wall that isn't a door. They drift aside every so often, gusting like plant fronds while you peer into the black hole beneath. Nothing happens but you keep sitting, your hair in wet rags, listening to what pass for love songs on some terrible radio through the chalk-scrape of interference. Waiting for Marilyn.

You never asked for her. Didn't, now you think, even know what her name was till the third appointment but that's whose you are. The receptionist says so: a child-woman with black-rimmed eyes and the fringe like rotten teeth, a breast or a target shaved into the stubble on her head and a smile like a meat slice. Marilyn's, aren't you? the purple stuff on her lips creasing. She smiles that way even when you don't look. Especially when you don't look. It means she knows. Even if you don't she does. You're definitely Marilyn's.

Walk this way.

You follow holding the loose ties of the pinny they gave you, not able to remember from last time how it's meant to do up, hoping nobody's looking. Only one free basin. Tomato-soup red and white checks appear in the mirror as you hove into view, your hands the wrong way round tying a double knot. Trying not to feel like someone's grandma, a trattoria table, you sit, take the towel when it's offered, wait as you're told. When you lower your neck down to where the sink might be, the muscles in your belly take the strain, levelling you backwards gently. The cold enamel bites at the warmth under the hairline. It sucks like a mouth. But the other feeling, a low excitement, carries on. Something that might be called butterflies. Through the mid-Atlantic Glasgow dj roaring for Sonja's seventeenth CONGRATS AND MIND HOW YOU GO OUT THERE SONJA, through the start of a tune that files your fillings, even when the shower touches first time. Through the repeated strokes of cool water you can still feel it fluttering, swallowing like a fish. The sensation of waiting. Waiting for Marilyn.

Nothing past the fringing.

The junior goes through shouting for Rita. You don't know the junior's name but she washed your hair, wrapped it wet inside the towel, twisting it too tight. You would have said but she wasn't looking. She didn't speak either, just walked you across the floor holding your arm like you were frail or fragile, taking tiny, footbound steps to the middle chair. The seat was burst, stitches big as bite marks over the open red gash: a trail of wet dots tagged your heels like a stray. You settled yourself over the healing plastic scar and waited some more. You wait still, watching the doorless hole gape and close, appear and fold itself away again behind the tease of strips. They nudge a little in the heat-haze while you wait, seeping, feeling the towel threaten to

74

lose its anchor and fall to the floor. But you take a risk anyway, peer round.

On the left, the slatted muzzles of strung-up dryers grunt soundlessly behind two copper-coloured cans of spray. Net on a wire rope hides the misted window. On the right, four women ranged along the wallpaper stripes, frying. Under their electric drying hoods, wisps of silver and lilac stray down, making their faces pucker. Their hands turn pages, making dry sounds, louder than the radio. Half-price day for over 60s. She said that the first time: We don't get many youngsters on a Wednesday, easing a scarlet comb down the back of your neck: I'm lucky to get you. Drawing the wet strands past your shoulders, checking its balance, her hands tucking under the sleek sheets. Then someone behind caught your eye, watching, and you turned away, waiting for the scissors, her tug on separate tresses. You recall the thud of a curl on your wrist, its slithering coolness. Your breath drawing in.

Rita's

The sign flashes on and off backwards from this side of the glass.

Same chip on the formica ledge.

Scarlet clamps, coils of cable snaking along the hairy floor, slit-faced socket boards in the skirting. But the plastic strips do not part. Anything that moved was only the junior, hauling one of the row out from under her smoked Perspex. We're ready to take your rods out now, Mrs Dixon. Mrs Dixon smiles and is easily led. The three women left behind don't even notice. One is asleep: the last merely holds a magazine, staring. It takes a moment before you realise she has no option. She can't close her eyes because the curlers under the hood stretch her skin too tight. Water makes a sheen over her eyes, a runnel to the cotton wool at the rim of the scarf. Someone slips past with a mug of coffee that is not for her. She watches it, goes back to the magazine. The phone starts and no-one goes. Mrs Dixon says thank you three times through repeated, unanswered ringing, the dj howling like a bitch in a shut room. This is his ALL-TIME FAVOURITE, his RED HOT TIP FOR THE TOP. You turn away, lower your shoulders. Black rubber teats appear. They're attached to a hair-dryer and you've no idea what they're for. You are still watching them when it happens. Something clicks.

Metal against metal.

Marilyn is there in the mirror, mouthing hello. Your skull tilting in her hands and Marilyn looking in the glass, checking you over with her fingertips.

Right we are, she says, lifting a comb from nowhere you can see. The usual? Marilyn lowering the scarlet teeth. Just tidy you up a wee bit, then?

A tug sears then relaxes, burning at the roots.

Yes, you say, just the same.

And she smiles and concentrates, the tip of her tongue appearing as she combs out your hair, wondering how much she'll take off.

That much ok?

The burr in the voice when she settles her hand on your shoulder to promise no more than an inch, you'll hardly notice. Her breath scented with milk. No more than an inch.

She steps back to begin and you can see what she's wearing today. Shorts and a loose shirt. Khaki. Things you wouldn't dare. Not knowing what to do with your hands, you watch her, Marilyn in army colours, raking her fingertips through the dead and drowned extremes of your being. It is you she handles with such seriousness, something you made from within your own body, opening the scissors carefully, bearing down and smiling to let you know it's ok. It's ok. Her familiar whisper. You're starting to relax when you see it. Something small glittering at the roots of her fingers. One finger. She sees you looking before you have time to cover up.

Engagement ring, she says. It's a real diamond.

The material of her shorts crushes against your arm.

I like solitaires.

A shear and flutter.

Marilyn is cutting your hair.

Marilyn with her slim hand hooped to some absent man.

Yes, you say. You have to say something. I didn't think.

But you do. A man in this choking female interior. Greased-back hair and a square jaw, solid. What kind of man? A pale mouth swallowing one of Marilyn's tiny breasts. You can't work out what this is washing over you like iced water, whether you're jealous. Of whom. The backs of his hands wrapping her thin white thighs before his hips move. The cushion he would make of her. Hoping so loud you almost speak. I hope he's not heavy.

Sorry? she says. Half her face turns pale blue.

Sorry?

Marilyn's slip of a girlness wondering what it was you said. Is everything ok? And you say, of course, laughing to make it truer. Looking down to hide the blush that's starting, you see the shorts leg wide of her skin, the way the cloth lifts to make a tunnel at her thigh. Wide enough for hand to slip inside. Just talking to myself.

Big blue eyes that haven't a clue what you're saying.

She smiles, her teeth perfect points, resumes.

The finger glitters as she tilts your head forward. A split-second of your own face, expressionless, appears as you go down, shutting its eyes again to wait for her touch on the nape of your neck.

The smug bastard on the radio keeps going.

Rita's

flashes backwards from the other side of the glass.

hope

The dark, the light, the dark.

The cartilage on either side of my little fingers. Blood bursting the capillaries in my nose rendering it warm. This is my face. My face. These are my palms on my cheeks like paper against more paper: four sheets. If I move them I will be able to see. I will be able to peek between first and second knuckle joint and see her. Still there. On the sofa opposite me, Hope. There is nothing surprising in that: it is where she always sits. Lies. Tonight she will most probably be lying down; lying down and not knitting. She will be lying down reading because it is the day her magazine comes. Every Thursday, the same magazine, one with advertisements and home decoration tips, how-I-coped stories. She reads it all evening, taking her time, snapping squares from a bar of chocolate. Other nights, she knits and watches tv: both at the same time. Tonight, though, she'll be lying on the sofa, sucking chocolate with her shoes off, the seams on the soles of her tights showing because this is her home. Home. A place you can unwind, let yourself go a little because you feel safe, in the bosom of your loved ones. A place you can be yourself. From where I sit, the magazine will obscure her face so I won't be able to admire it. What I will see are wisps of hair, her painted nails, tulips behind her head in a glass vase. I will be able to admire those instead. Red hair, red nails, red tulips with black hearts; concentric circles going round the handmade rug;

Victorian washbasin on the windowsill; cottage prints, frills on the curtains. She uses decorating tips in the magazine so it's not money wasted. Doing things to the house gives her an outlet. She calls it that herself, an outlet. That and the poems. Hope writes poems. You need a hobby she says, hobbies are relaxing, they give you a sense of who you are and writing poems is hers. She encourages me in the same way, says I need a hobby too and she may be right. I work too much she says: working at home can do that. I work at home balancing other people's books. My own boss, hours I can fit round our life together instead of the other way round: all plus side, she says. Not only that but we have the constant reassurance the other is near. Constant. Not many people are so lucky she says, especially not people with children. We do not have children so we have the time to be truly together in a way most couples can only dream about. That is what we are doing now. The cats are in our bed upstairs and Hope is at rest in the sofa, reading her magazine. Though I can't see them, I know her poet's eyes are behind the cigarette carton on the back cover, glossing the promises of skin creams and home gardening tips, suggestions to improve her love life. Unless, of course, she has them closed. Even if my own eyes were open, I would not be able to tell for sure, not from this angle. I would, however, be able to regard her feet: vulnerable little feet inside nylon casings with blood-coloured nails glinting through the orange mesh. I would be forced to notice her nails match the tulips too. And if I looked down, if I turned my head, my own feet would appear. Slippered. On the rug. I peer through my fingers and there they are, my feet in blue tartan wrappers. I watch them double and blur, fade back into themselves again, my fingers pressing deep into the soft cave of my sockets before my eyelids reclose. They close because I cannot stop them. And the vision comes again: the same vista playing uninvited on the screen of my closed eyelids, the same vision every time. Mile after mile of empty rail-track, the moss on its sleepers deep as velvet. Mile after mile rolling between broken stone and sky. A place no train has passed for years or is likely to come again, where no-one will pass by, wave or turn to notice me. On either side, burned-out fields and wasteground that roll to the horizon are barren and roadless, a forgotten wild where no-one offers kindness, a meal on a clean tablecloth, a brow I can kiss. If I try I can feel the chill of the place slicing my coat, its scissoring wind: the almost palpable scour of sand between my teeth. And then, when I am on the verge of moaning aloud with pleasure, she catches me. She calls me back. Hope coughing. A sound she could not help but still. I press my fingers hard into the closed lids, trying not to know. The darkness, pain through the swollen skin. I push harder, heart pounding.

She coughs again.

Before long I will get up and offer to make tea. If I don't, she will come over. She will reach and pat my hand. Can't I be at peace tonight? Never mind. She will pat my hand, rearrange my shirt collar. I need more time off, she'll say. I ought to relax more. I smoke too much. I overwork.

On the other side of the room, I hear the crushing of the chocolate wrapper, the smacking of lips. Hope's sweet little mouth getting ready to offer me a kiss.

Sooner or later. I will have to open them.
Sooner or later I will have to open my eyes.

bisex

I worry.
Sometimes I need to hear your voice.

I worry. I phone.
You are often out when I phone.

I walk to the far end of the kitchen and hold the kettle under the tap, watch the red marker on the side rise on the fresh water. You could be shopping but not this late: a concert maybe, a show. Walking somewhere, backstreets under the streetlamps, the park no-one would go to the park at night, the middle of the town. I have no way of knowing. The pictures then, the sauna trying not to think the sauna. The kettle is half-full. Four cups. The sauna. I switch the tap off with one hand, bracing the muscles in the other for the weight of carrying, turn away from my reflection in the window, the rictus of polished jars behind the sink.

Three bags left. Three white purses pooling brown dust. That means six cups of tea if I'm careful. Six for one. I replace the blue and white lid so I don't have to think about there being less now and dowse the first square, fighting it back under with the stream of boiling water every time it tries to surface, then coax it with the spoon before fishing it into another cup for later. I'm running out of milk. Just enough so the tea turns cloudy auburn, seeping from the unmixed splash of white. Greyish white. The kitchen table, the hot cylinder between my hands. The sauna a disco or pub a pub always the same ones. Always. The same ones. Eyes closed, rubbing my mouth against the cup. Even when it burns I don't pull away.

You.

You reach across the table.

There is a glass with a slice of lemon, bubbles gathering like spawn along the rim. Your hand lays stripes on the frosted bowl. Your hand. It lifts the glass, settles it against your mouth momentarily, puts it back in exactly the same place. Holding a glass for no reason is what I do, not you. It's near an ashtray, stubbed with butts. Your hair is only just too long, blond creeper over the collar of your jacket at the back. At the front it makes spikes in your eyes. Between that and the smoke in here you can hardly see. Hair in your eyes, booze and no specs not even any sign of the specs. Little vanities leave you wide open. Regardless, you lift the glass again, sip. The way you swallow, jerk the plumbline of that maleness in your throat is smooth, practised. The way you settle the glass back, running your finger and thumb the length of its stem, watching it fizz.

My stomach dips.

Someone is pulling into focus behind the crook of your arm where it lifts, fetches a cigarette to your mouth. The arm stays flexed, waiting for someone to offer a match. I can't tell if you know he is there, whether you move knowing you are observed or not. In any case, he approaches while you strike and pout, inching the cigarette for the flame the way I've seen you do it a hundred times, eyes puckering up when you draw and his hand touches the table. Your table. You peer at the nameless hand, flicking your head to clear your vision, inhaling, blowing the match out with the first breath of smoke. And you let him sit. You raise your eyes slowly, blowing the match dead. You always let him sit.

And I don't know. I don't know how you begin with these men.

After the shared silences, the contact that implies nothing and everything, messages that could be retracted as soon as understood, after you approach each other, how the real game starts. How you admit to each other what you are doing, whether there is no need. Euphemism and hedging, daring to meet his eyes for whole seconds, tipping your tongue against your carefully white teeth. You play games you would not begin to play with me, risking everything and nothing, waiting for a sign. And sooner or later it comes, though neither of you will be able to say afterwards when that moment was or how it was reached. A change in the temperature of the shared glances, maybe. Or he could simply say it out loud. I don't know. I don't know how it is decided, the rising to leave together, how you choose: whether tonight it's you or him who stands up first. Whether you have somewhere to go, whether you wait while he finishes a drink and wipes his mouth or whether you leave and he follows. His strange scent tracking you down, maybe knowing somewhere warm and safe. Whether it is only the bus shelter or back street, opened coats and the press of concrete at your back. Whether you touch first or he does. I wonder and try not to think, thinking anyway. Either way, there are always folds of cloth. I always see folds of cloth.

Your hand stretching across the drapery of his jeans to his belt, your fingers lifting the buckle to slip the leather. Blond fingers, taut with muscle, white as mushroom stalks free the buckle and find the zip, a single nail running the length of closed teeth towards the tag to inch it down. Your lips part and your eyelids are closed. Already, your breath fractures as you reach inside. His fingers reach for your shirt buttons.

What happens then is less distinct. It's you I want to see. Falling blond, the fringe lapping the closed lids as his fist accelerates and your mouth opens, that catch in your breath. His lips cover yours, the scratch of stubble on your cheek something familiar, something fond. And I envy that kiss, this tenderness. The thick vein that I have trailed with my tongue courses inside his fist. It pulses for him. His grip stronger than mine.

And when it's finished, after you share a sameness with him and your hands lace, sticky, I worry about what it is you say. Whether you touch him the way you touch me. I don't want to think they spend the night, these pickups something stinging in the crease of my mouth these pickups and strangers. Yet I don't want to think of you alone. It feels terrible to think of you alone, smoking in cafes and bars, waiting. I do not want you to be alone. And I know somewhere deeper that's all you want too. What I imagine is nothing as real as that longing, as what you're really looking for. The thing that is not, will never be me. The feeling of coming home.

Should be more careful. Almost drop the cup.

It's cold now anyway, unpleasant to touch. Only fit for throwing away. I notice the crack on the rim when I cross to the sink, the red stain there. Little red trail against the eggshell blue. When I put my hand up to my face there's more. My mouth is bleeding. I rinse the cup, wipe my mouth, turn off the tap. Dark as hell out there: the guttering and dead leaves breaking off their branches. Steam growing from my breath against the pane. Trying not to think too much. Not to worry.

I need to talk to you.

I try not to reach for the phone.

peeping tom

I don't always see him.

The front door's quiet and I put the radio on the minute I get in so I don't always know he's back till he shouts. Then I turn the volume down, listen. Shoes clonking on the floor, the shiver of a shirt coming off. Bedroom. He's up the other end of the hall, in the bedroom. YOOHOO, I shout. I'm in the kitchen. He knows. I know he knows. He must have passed me on the way in but I like to shout anyway, be a presence. Now we both know where the other one is. Something comes back, an acknowledgement maybe. Either that or he's bumped into something through there. A kind of squeaky noise. I smile in case it's meant for me, turn back and get on with the pizza.

First pizza I ever ate was out of the Tally cafe at the corner of the main road, just across from Bobby's Amusement Arcade. We'd go in there after a night on the puggies and get a pizza supper between two. The big woman would chuck the pizza in the chip fat whole and it surfaced with the bread dough more or less transparent. Those days we had some kind of supper out the cafe every Saturday without thinking twice. Usually fish but with the occasional foray into the more exotic so eventually I'd tried the whole range: black pudding, chicken, sausage, hamburger, haggis, curry, chow mein, lasagna and pie. I only got the pie once. They got fried whole as well. The curry and chow mein were done in batter parcels like big spring rolls, envelope-ended.

Godknew how they did the lasagna. I never heard anybody else ask for it but it was always there, on the menu board. Fryer Tuck's they called it. Fryer Tuck's. If there was any Italian connection they were keeping it to themselves. The chips were variable. Sometimes ok, other times slimy from the double wrapping, flaccid and sweetish with frying sweat. The longer you left them in their enclosed environment, the worse shape they'd be in when they came out. We got them anyway. Every time. It wasn't anything to do with the taste, it wasn't even that we were that hungry. Mostly it was to keep warm. I lived a long walk back from the stance, last bus and everything. He had to walk all the way back to the other side of town on his own. He always took me though, walked me home nomatter what the weather was like. If it was really cold, the fat congealed on our fingers, clung there like vaseline. I remember one night it was snowing, him holding a hand up to the streetlamp: five fingers splayed against the light, a thick fur of condensation round the bulb casing. He just held it there, sort of peering, clueless. He'd nothing to wipe them on. So I gave him something. I gave him me. Took his hand in mine and sucked it, all the salt and leftover slickness, one digit at a time. He knew exactly what I was doing. When I shoved him against the haulage contractor's wall just round the corner from Springvale Street he was ready. So was I. Dropped on my hunkers and took his prick in my mouth whole, one go. Sheer greed. I remember his breath turning to white cloud, spilling down over my shoulders. I can even taste him if I think hard enough, Roddy and leftover brackishness from the pickle skin. I have a memory like godknows. Ok it wasn't all that comfortable but it couldn't have taken longer than five minutes. Not long enough to get cramp. Afterwards, his jacket was pitted with pebbles from the roughcast, my knees rusted over with cold. He rubbed them till I could walk straight again and we went back, the two of us laughing like drains. My mother caught us kissing on the doorstep and acted shocked. Maybe she was. Mothers and daughters. There you go.

Tonight we're having pizza because he's in a hurry. I'm hoping he won't know the difference if it's yeasted or not. He's running a bath through there, drawers opening and shutting. He doesn't shout through or ask what's for tea. He locks the door.

How was your day? I shout through.

There's flour all over my hands, wee misty trails drifting down to the dark blue carpet while I'm shouting.

What? It's muffled through water noise and the layers of chip board. But he's heard me ok. Are you saying something out there?

I said, how was your day?

Fine, he says. How was your day?

So so. Well. Tell you the truth, some of it was terrible.

Yelling sends shock waves up my arms and a tiny piece of dough shakes loose. It drops from someplace I don't see and lands, a crescent in the night sky, on the dark pile. I look at my hands again, the dust filtering down.

I'm just going to wash my hands, I say. Ok? I'm making a big mess out here, then wait in case he wants to answer. All I hear is wee splashes. I go back to the kitchen with one hand cupped under the other, bolting the stable door. The flour just keeps falling through. Back in the kitchen I hear he's turned the tap on again, topping up. He likes a long soak.

Used to be as soon as I heard running water, I'd start shelling clothes. I loved getting in there with him, creaming up the soap then rubbing the lather from my hands over his shoulders and chest. We could spend ages, him making soap bubbles between my breasts while I dipped my fists under the water level, working till he poked out the water like a rhubarb shoot. After a while it was harder to find the time. New shift system and everything. I'M HAVING A BATH TO GET CLEAN FOR GODSAKE MOIRA he'd say I'M IN A HURRY. It wasn't just that though. I think he got shy because of this new stuff they started using on the plant, stuff that stank so he came home with it all through his hair, in places you couldn't imagine how it got there. He still left the door open, let me wander through and chat. I liked watching all that lean muscle, the way he could bend in the middle without triple rolls of fat appearing. Not long after he got on the overtime roster though, he took to snibbing the door. It was the only way to avoid temptation and anyway a man needs his privacy. You've all night to take baths, he says: some of us haven't. And it's perfectly true. He hasn't.

These days you get pizza topping ready made. It comes in jars with the garlic already in, herbs as well if you want them. You can get bases too but I still do my own. Even if it's just scone, my bases are all home-made. I put this one on a baking tray, stick on some of the jar stuff and add extra tomato, sliced yellow pepper, flakes of tuna. I'm just cutting a big chunk of cheddar for the grater when I hear the lock release, the pad of freshly-minted feet. He puts stuff like the filling out of After-Eights on them to get rid of the factory smell. He goes away through to the bedroom on these perfectly edible feet with one towel round his waist, another over his shoulders to catch the drips from his hair. His hair looks black when it's freshly washed though it's really ash brown. It looks black at least once a day. I can see wee slices of him from here, like a row of coins through the louvres of the room divider, combing back the wet hair, laying out a row of mousse and hair gel, deodorant, talc, aftershave. He bends his knees to use the hair dryer, trying to see in a mirror angled for my height. After a minute he goes back through to the bathroom. Hiding. He knows I'm looking. I go back round to the worktop and twist the lid off a jar of gherkins trying to look if he's checking I've taken the hint and something sears my finger. There's a cut, a clean white incision fanning red threads through the whorl on my fingertip. Cut myself and didn't notice. The evidence is there, wee scarlet patches through the grated cheese when I look. I'll need to do everything else with one useless finger tucked into the palm. The plasters are in the bathroom. Behind my back I hear the oven light change from red to amber, the timer humming.

Fifteen minutes, I shout. Roddy? Your tea's up in fifteen minutes, you hear? knowing he won't have. That door's as good as soundproof. He won't have heard a bloody word.

After mine, I watch the news. It's what I always do. There's something about the seven o'clock news that's reassuring: the way it goes on for ages, does repeats of the main bulletins to make sure you've heard it all as though they really care. Jon Snow, all velvet voice and silk tie, tells me about food mountains and the hard Ecu, his adam's apple rising and dipping above a cool white collar. His eyes are so blue they're not real. By the time he's doing industrial streamlining, Roddy's voice slips over my shoulder in a haze of aftershave.

Something smells good.

He means the pizza. I know he means the pizza. I turn round ready to say, It must be you then, in a kind of sexy way for a joke and he's not there. He's in the hall. His elbow pokes out the junk cupboard, the rest of him in there wrestling to get by the hoover.

I've had mine. Shouting again. Yours is in the kitchen.

Sorry?

Pizza. I'm roaring. Your tea. It's in the kitchen.

Keep it for me ok? Hangers rattling. A thump. Christ, who put all this shit in here, Moira.

He's out the cupboard. The last word, that MOIRA, is louder so he's definitely out the cupboard.

Got the paper? There are jacket noises now, scuffling. Good movie on later. I saw it in the canteen.

Oh?

I forget the name of it now but it's a good one. You always say you've seen them but you haven't seen this. You should watch it.

What time?

Eh?

What time's it on?

Late. Late film.

Well. I don't know. I'm dead tired. Unless you want to see it. I had a terrible day.

Cmon Moira I'll not be in. You know fine. It's Tuesday. I'm never in on Tuesday.

Oh. When will you be home?

I won't disturb you ok?

When will you be home?

You won't even know I'm back.

Roddy? When will you —

The door clicks.

Beethoven. Not long after eight, the van comes round. The first eight of *Für Elise* buggered about to sound like a tune on a Waltzer but it means there are crisps and ice-cream, packets of fags if anybody's dying for them. Sometimes I'm in that state myself but not tonight. Not in the mood for the queue. Anyway, hearing it reminds me to pull the curtains, put on the wee lamp. Then I look back at the telly. There's never anything decent on at this time of night but I always flick through the channels just in case. After a couple of goes I give in, switch off and start rearranging furniture. It's not a big room but you can make space: it rearranges fine. Some evenings I do that. I clear a bit of space and do yoga. I wear black tights and a leotard, leg-warmers. Used to yoga all the time only there was less of me then. Moira, he would say, watching me stretch, you're all woman. I still fit the same stuff but I only put it on when he's out. Kitted up, I come down the hall again avoiding the mirror, hooking in the dangly ear-rings blind. I like to wear dangly ear-rings when I'm doing yoga. It makes me feel more exotic, as though I know what I'm doing. They brush your neck when you roll your head from side to side, feel like someone's fingers. All the rooms off the hall are in darkness. In the livingroom I put on the fire, sit in front of the real-effect flames and select something for the turntable. First thing that comes to hand is an old one. *Great Love Ballads of our Time*. There's some crap on it but at least it's slow crap. You need the right tempo for this kind of thing, helps keep the heart rate steady. Annie Lennox comes on, her voice all alone, then chiming bells. Carefully, I put on the headphones. I turn the music loud enough to block out my own breathing and I'm ready.

Steady.

I brace my shoulders so my chest pushes out, my stomach in. The bass line throbbing through the carpet pile makes a direct line to my crotch. Time to begin.

Kneel. Lean back till my hair starts folding under itself on the fireside rug, lower torso from the hips, rest. Once that feels ok, inch lower still, resting elbows on the floor to take some of the weight before flattening my back against the carpet. Rest. Legs bent double, feet cushioning my backside, I look down. All I can see are my breasts making roadsigns, twin humpback bridges. All woman. Rest long enough and the pain reaches one even note; disused muscles taking the strain, trying to accommodate. Then the last. I close my eyes for concentration then arch my spine, bracelet my ankles with my hands. I'm there. Bowed like a bridge, a perfect camber, I open my eyes. There's a man at the french window. Looking in.

Hardly anyone comes on the landing.
He knocks, hat dipping over the eyes.
A policeman.

It means only one thing.

1. They found a van covered with blood at the side of the road, a man several yards away. He staggered free and tried to reach a call box, one foot attached only by rags of skin. He's out cold but his diary gave them this address. The name in the diary is

2. There's been a head-on collision with a drunk driver. The drunk is absolutely fine. They tried to cut the other man out of his van but he's still there. They're having to amputate to free him so he can't be given anaesthetic. He's asking for someone called Moira at this address. The man's name appears to be

3. An overtaking lorry crushed a van into the crash barriers on the motorway. Every bone in the driver's body is broken. They don't expect him to last the night. There is nothing they can give him to reduce the pain. He screams himself out of unconsciousness and mutters our phone number every so often. He answers to the name of

4. To avoid a child on the road, a van driver swerved, skidded and drove straight into a tree. Smashed glass has made him unrecognisable and the steering wheel has pushed right through his ribcage. His eyes have been

Jesus.

Christ.

Before I've worked out how to do it, I'm out of position and racing for a dressing gown then I'm at the door. The policeman is calm. He says nothing awful. He even smiles. Routine checks madam, just routine checks. I'm catching my breath but so he doesn't notice, trying to look collected, calm. According to him this is a man's flat he says. So it is, I say, smiling back.

He just looks at me.

It is a man's flat, I say. I'm just a decoration.

He looks at me again. Pardon?

It's ok, I say. I'm being smartarsed, and he laughs. We both laugh. I live here too.

He comes in, sits down while I float back and forth with peach towelling bunched at my waist, leggings showing to the thigh. I invite him to take off his hat, brassy as you like. He wipes the single drops of rain off the brim with a slow, thick hand, sits back. He asks me to sit too. He's here to tell me something. There are Peeping Toms, he says. Three complaints from my block. I stop then, look directly at him. His raincoat smells so fresh it might be flowers. Big hands clutching the edge of the settee.

Roddy told me he wanted to be a songwriter. He couldn't play any instruments and wasn't learning any, but he wanted to be a songwriter. You would meet such interesting people that way, he said. Then he fancied lorry driving, cruising through the dark with hands steady on the wheel, watching the world with seen-it-all eyes, carrying explosives/nuclear waste/Yorkie Bars with slit-skirted girls thumbing lifts at the side of the road. Then he wanted to be an art student, a sound technician, a vet. He even wanted to be a policeman when he found out they got a house with the job. The apprenticeship at the petrochemical plant came up just when I was enjoying the idea of him in uniform. That's not now though. That has nothing to do with now. I can't think why I thought it. Right now, the policeman is talking to me. His notebook is tucked under his thigh. I raise my eyes slowly and tell him I've seen nothing. Nothing at all.

Anyone new in the area, recently? Hanging around the lifts or shops downstairs?

No, I say. Just in and out to work, you don't notice much. I wouldn't have noticed anyone old round here, never mind anyone new.

He nods, looks round. Nice flat.

Yes, I say. So my mother keeps telling me.

He makes a sort of smile, refuses an offer of tea. We say nothing for a moment while he keeps looking round.

Well, he says. He takes a deep breath in. Sorry if I called at an – eh – inconvenient moment.

I look down at the dressing gown belt, the big bumphle in the knot and try to look casual. That's ok, I say. Come again any time.

Right, he says. Haha. And he starts walking towards the door.

Sure you don't want tea? I say.

Quite sure, he says. You're very kind.

And before I know what I'm doing, it comes out.

There's pizza, I say. I hear myself saying it.

He stops, turns round. His eyes are dark brown.

Home-made pizza. It's just going to waste through there. You can have a piece.

I tilt my head.

If you like.

Two seconds. That's all it takes. And he's on the other side of the door before either of us sees how he got there. He looks back briefly, reminds me from the safety of the front porch if I see anything suspicious I'm not to hesitate to call.

I won't, I say.

He's already away down the stairs so I'm talking to the closed door. I tell it again for good measure.

I won't.

The headphones are still on the carpet when I go back through, playing to the skirting. I hold them to one ear. *When I Fall in Love*, Nat

104

King Cole. So I put the damn thing off. Two cups, one untouched, go
into the sink. I stick the uneaten pizza in the oven so it's there if Roddy
wants it when he comes in, then close every curtain in the house.
Tight. After that it's just me and the late-night movie, the livingroom
light full on. I stare hard at the screen, trying to look totally absorbed,
seeing nothing. All I can think about is some bastard up on the roof
looking for gaps in the breeze block. Crazed with loneliness but jesus
christ. The telly stays on till the dot appears, a silence then that horrible
execution drum roll and the Queen on a horse. Somehow that's
worse. It's worse than the silence, listening to the national anthem in
the flat at night: like a setup from one of those films where some
woman gets disembowelled with a tin-opener just when she thinks
she's safe and sound in her own place. I read somewhere thinking like
that is an easy option. Women these days should refuse to fall for that
easy victim mentality it said. So I snap the red button on the remote
control fast, brave nothingness instead. It's not better but it's not
worse. I walk down the hall practising a brave face, refusing to be a
victim. At least then I'll know if I'm raped and hacked to fragments I
didn't give the guy any encouragement. I didn't ask for it. I want to be
sure I took no chances on that score.

The bathroom is the only room with no windows. I undress in
there tonight, put the dressing gown back on before checking the
house again. I have to put the porch light on for Roddy: the hall is dark
as hell. I go down it, patting the walls to find my way, stroking the
sleek white plaster I'm so proud of. This is my home. A catch on the
new estate. Everybody said so: seven power points in the livingroom
and central heating. Central heating, my mother said. Don't know
they're born these days. I think she was pleased. She never said things
directly, my mother, nothing nice anyway but you knew. Don't know
they're born. I remember she was standing at the far side of the stereo
cabinet when she said it, rain-mate on. There were beads of rain

caught between the folds of sheer plastic that did not fall. It smelled like clean. The whole place smelled like clean. She brought white sheets for a moving-in present, white sheets in cellophane. I'm remembering all this. I can hear the sheets for christsake, Roddy laughing. And suddenly it's all so clear, so sharp I need to stop and get my breath back. When I look up again I'm leaning against the wall, cheek squashed against the white surface. I'm embracing the wall and my face is wet. It only lasts a moment though. A moment then I'm fine, right as rain. I dust myself down just in case anybody was watching, reach for the porch switch. No faces loom from the dark, nothing sounds. I wipe my face with the back of one hand, tell myself I'm fine. Moira, you're perfectly fine.

Between the sheets before I take the dressing gown off.
Funny how nervous you can get.

The rattle of his keyring comes eventually.

I hear him easing the key back into the lock on the inside, the tumblers being primed for the early start tomorrow. Then the hollow suckings of shoes being removed, stocking soles whispering towards the kitchen. The fridge hums when he opens the door, seeing what there is for late supper while the pizza sits ignored in the oven. He won't even know it's there. After a minute or two, he scuffles out of his clothes, runs water to wash and brush his teeth in the dark so he doesn't disturb me. He's always been thoughtful that way. He sighs, slips in beside me cautious as a cat then gently draws against my back, pressing his knees behind mine so we curve like spoons. It's warm; a good, good feeling. It's so good I want to turn, embrace him. I don't want to tell him about the policeman or the rotten day I've had, just hold him. But I can't. Instead I pretend to roll in my sleep, touch his hip lightly with one hand, hoping he'll reach back. He's wearing his underwear.

Sorry, he says. Sorry, too tired tonight.
He turns away, pushes his backside against mine.

Before long, I hear him snoring gently, mouthing empty air.

My eyes are wide open, watching for Peeping Toms.

babysitting

Something he can't see hurts.

He kneels on the floor to pick up the fallen shell of flying saucer and it bites into his knee, making a noise. A soft, spreading crack. Wondering if it was bone, your own bone maybe being drilled into by something very small. He lifts the knee to look and it's sugar. Little clear cubes sunk up to their middles, the skin pushing them out again with stretching over the kneecap. Skin is like that. Mushy. Things get stuck in it. Gads. The sugar bounces out of its burrows, skites on the lino: more of it scattered over the rest of the floor. It would be Allan did that. Allan in at the packet again and spilling it. A white trail coming out the cupboard to here proves it. Tommy watches it with his eye all the way. Where it stops is just sticky powder. The place the knee was seconds before. A drift of it silts in at the wood under the sink as well. And something else. Something with legs. A wispy black thing moves threads of itself against the skirting, a bead-string of a body rising up then away again, back underneath. He looks till his sore eye starts to nip but it's definitely away, just slivers of biscuit and crumby stuff left, papery shapes that onions leave all over the place. You see more things down here. Things you don't really want to see all that much. Anyway the knee isn't sore any more. It's got holes in. Pock marks. Most of the sugar has worked its way out without him even trying. He picks out the last bits with a nail. This filthy nail, black-rimmed where the horn separates from the quick, the loops of

111

fingerprint grey. The blood bruise is still there. Going yellow. At least it isn't a cigarette burn. They go brown.

Tommy?

A whine and a sniff is coming closer. The boy on the floor doesn't move.

Tommy?

The last bit of sugar gouges itself out the knee as the sniff blossoms out, rounding the hall corner. Allan.

Tommy?

Allan with his voice breathy, just the same. It never changes, the way he says your name, whether he thinks he knows where you are or not, not even when he finds you. He always sounds as if he's going to moan about something. The warm bulk of the wee brother sends out signals and Tommy knows what he's going to say. Starving. Is it teatime. It's what he always says. Yesterday he kept it up till they went and took some of the money for penny things: toffee straps, licorice ropes. Flying saucers. Allan ate them all in a oner and his face was black. The other day he was behind the settee with four sweetie cigarettes and it was ages before you found out where he'd got them. Finally he said David Armstrong from up the stairs gave them to him through the letterbox and you had to take them off him and fling them in the bin. He shouldn't have been taking things from David Armstrong. He was told not to take things off anybody. David Armstrong was bad enough. Him putting stuff through the letterbox was worse, though. Tommy didn't know why but it was definitely not good. He had to prop a chair in front of the door to stop the flap going up again or Allan opening it from his side and shouting through. Being so wee, you had to watch him all the time. Putting the chair there and just giving him a battering every so often was easier than trying to talk sense because he was too wee to do what he was told and be trusted. Even obvious things like not talking to Mrs Morrison. You just didny talk to Mrs Morrison. She just got you into trouble. Somebody kicked her door once and she said it was Tommy and dad told her to fuck off and then you caught Allan talking to her. She was a Nosy Old Cow and she gave you gyp. He'd been told but it had taken the leathering to get it through. Allan just hadny a clue.

Tommy?

Allan is there, fat inside the doorway holding an empty crisp poke. One leg of the trainer bottoms up at his knee and the sock needing pulled up.

Is it teatime Tommy?

A flake of crisp falls off the corner of Allan's fat mouth and in with the rest of the bits on the floor. His nose running, coating his top lip. Sometimes you want to thump Allan for nothing. He just gets on your nerves. Anyway Tommy gets up. He peels his knees off the lino and sees the sugar again but he doesn't say anything. He just starts walking. He walks through to the hall, past the living room door and through to the bedroom window, listening to Allan follow him. Allan's feet skiffing off the carpet. When Tommy stops, he does too. Just stands there clueless, crumpling the crisp poke over and over in thon irritating way while his brother looks out.

The sky is grey and pink.

No streetlights on yet but too hard to see right inside the house any more. There is a time when it is harder to see before it gets easier and it is that time the now. When it gets darker, the orange sifts in from out there and you don't need to put the inside lights on at all: you can see ok without them. Anyway they only ever go through to the living-room and the telly is on in there. You can see it fine without lights or anything. He can hear it, still going full bung, making shouting noises and car brakes through the wall. Tommy can hear it fine. But it wouldn't be a good idea to stick Allan through when he went out for the tea. He didn't like it, being on his own with dad through there. He does it all right if you force him but not without a carry on. So Allan

113

will have to come too. Quicker in the long run. Tommy shuts his eyes and thinks about going out into the hall. About holding out one hand backwards and not having to wonder where Allan is. He is just always there, ready to take it. He will drop the crisp poke and fit his hand inside and let himself be taken. It's what Allan does. He needs watching.

David Armstrong looks like a ferret and hunches his shoulders up, looking over. He kicks the wall where the chippy is, holding a bag in the one hand. Maltesers.

How were you not at school the day?

David Armstrong talks like a lassie and nobody plays with him. He was never done out on his own, looking for folk. Tommy feels the eyes and refuses to look up, the crinkle of the sweetie bag in the other hand and keeps a good grip of Allan. David Armstrong always has something for eating but you're better off without it. Anything you got off David Armstrong was not good. Him and his mother both. You were better to tell them nothing. He would have given the sweetie cigarettes to Allan and then told his mother they'd been taken off him. He did things like that.

How no though?

The face a melted doll and the eyes watching. Able not to eat and just wait. He made you sick. One time they dug his rabbit up after it had been in the ground a week to see if it was any different and it wasn't only the eyes were kind of white and his mother caught him and he said it was Tommy and Allan. He said they made him do it and started greeting and that made his mother think it was true. You took nothing off him if you could help it. Tommy flexes his hand tighter, Allan's bone thin and hard through the cloth and soft flesh and he whines. He doesn't pull though. He whines a bit with the soreness in his arm but he doesn't try to go over. At their backs, David Armstrong shouting Fuck off then. Soft as rotten fruit.

Inside the chippy is warm. It is always warm and smells of food. Mrs Mancini sometimes gives Allan a free pickled onion. This time she just looks. She looks at Tommy and twists the salt shaker.

You two here again, she says. Her face isn't right. Bertie, these two are here again.

Mr Mancini looks over the top of the glass cabinet, thin straps of hair over his scalp. His face boils over a cabinet full of black puddings then goes away. Tommy holds up the three coins. Maybe they think he doesn't have the money. Nobody takes it. Nobody is looking because they are talking to each other, words he can't hear right: Mrs Mancini saying something about it being the umpteenth time, you wonder where the hell it's coming from the two of them twice a day and Tommy knows something. They're talking about him and Allan. And that doesn't feel good either. They should just get the food and get out. He wants to get back up the road and jam the chair back where it belongs. The back of the door is not safe when they're out like this. He wants home.

Fish supper and an extra bag.

He hears his own voice being sure about what he wants. Then they might get it and get out. Nobody can stop you if you have the money.

Fish supper and an extra bag.

Mr Mancini says something about nothing to do with him and the frying spits up. Tommy lifts his eyes. Mrs Mancini's hair appears over the top of the cabinet, the pink overall shifting into place behind the counter. She gives them a look.

Ok boys. Fish supper and an extra bag.

Her lipstick is a funny colour and doesn't smile. She takes the ladle out the pickles and stares at it. The chips come and she wraps them staring at where Mr Mancini must be. She picks up the newspaper bundle and reaches, still looking away.

See and say to your daddy I'm asking for him boys ok?

Ok. Allan is looking at the newspaper parcel, saying ok to Mrs Mancini. She claps eyes on him and stained teeth show. Marks on her teeth like a vampire.

You need your face washed young man, she says. See and wash his face if nobody else will.

The pink thing she wears moves when she leans, handing over the bags. Tommy nearly takes it then remembers sauce. Look at him Bertie he's completely mockit. He's filthy. Tommy doesn't listen and asks hard for sauce. She looks. She reaches to take the parcel back.

I don't know, she says. I don't know. A couple of chancers.

Fat fizzes up and more fish hurl themselves into the display case. Mrs Mancini holds out an opened palm for the money.

The house always feels colder after you've been out.

Tommy shivers through the shirt and reaches for the switch. Hard greasy plastic. It is not like real light that comes on. It makes things look sore. The wrapped bundle in at his chest, burning, he walks through to the kitchen. Hot vinegar hurts his nose. Allan follows close enough to tip the backs of his heels, the rubber bumpers of the trainers touching. In a minute there will be whining about wanting his bag. But there is something about the idea of washing his hands, cleaning Allan up a bit before he eats. He wants to make sure Allan looks ok. He puts the bags to one side of the sink where Allan can't reach and looks for the wet dish cloth. It isn't there. Tommy looks and the whining starts. The cloth isn't there. It isn't there because it's in the livingroom. The sound of the telly playing music and Allan starting to reach up for the bundle on the drainer. After. It'll have to be after. If Allan starts up now it'll be more bother than it's worth. Tommy watches the newspaper start to slide, Allan's face change as it falls into his grasp. He tears a bit off the end of the parcel and it nearly cowps. As soon as he gets the chips he'll want a drink. You were never done with Allan. He was always wanting something. They were nearly out of lemonade as well.

Cmon you. Cmon.

Tommy makes up his mind. He takes the chips before the whole lot falls and the greeting gets worse. They're not eating off the kitchen floor.

Cmon.

Any minute and the wail will start. But all he has to do is go through, look like he means it. Allan will follow. He always does. He runs.

Blotches.

The telly throws grey blobs over the inside of the room, shifting all the time. The sour smell. He holds the bags up to his nose for the vinegar stink off the newspaper to make it ok. And it is ok. It's always ok after a minute or so but you always notice the smell on the way in. Allan stumbles in grizzling then shuts up when he sees unwrapping going on. He never notices the stink. He never notices anything when he's hungry. Tommy hands him the extra bag and a piece of fish off his own. The fish is cool enough to tear easy without hurting your hand. Allan watches the trade of fish, bits flaking onto the carpet, then picks his bit up and sticks it to his mouth, chewing. Tommy knows what he forgot. Biscuits. There are no biscuits left and hardly any lemonade. Stuff just keeps going done. There's no sauce. It doesn't matter just now though. Just now, there are chips and sauce from the shop. It'll do. It'll have to.

From the far side of the divan, father's legs flash patterns: the news making spider webs. It makes the legs look as if they're moving but the feet are in exactly the same place. They never move. He might leave some chips in case though. Tommy bites the fish, looks down at the carpet. It looks as if it's moving as well, heaving about like the sea thon time they went the holiday, like something's living in it but it's still not time for the light yet. There are things you don't want to see when it's on. The yellow colour that keeps just getting yellower for a start. It is definitely getting darker since the start of this. Allan coughs suddenly and bits spray out but he keeps chewing. He's ok. The fat fingers glisten as the adverts change. After. He can get Allan through for a wash and into bed. It's getting too cold sleeping in here anyway, even with the two of them. That'll have to stop as well. After he's done with Allan, Tommy will come back through. He wants to sit for a bit. He needs to check for money in the pockets anyway. He wipes grease off his mouth, flicks his eyes away. It isn't nice to think about, raking the pockets. Having to touch him. It makes his mouth stop working, the chip mush in his throat stick. But he can make it quick. Then just sit, sit in with his own dad and maybe talk. Ask if he's ok. There's no point doing it out loud these days but he does it anyway. Even if he never says, you want to ask.

Inside the wrapper, the chips get colder. You see the fat on them going stiff. You know you don't want to lift his eyelids though. Touch the skin thickening there. You don't want to know the colour of his eyes.

someone had to

Blue eyes.

Right from the start her mother said, from the word go that was what people noticed. Took after her dad, she said: those big blue eyes, that LOOK on her. Not blinking. Fixed.

People sentimentalise; children and animals it's what they do. She may not speak much but she knows EVERY WORD YOU SAY. Her mother said that. Kind of thing you say about spaniels. Biddable things. Pets. They sentimentalise. It's easier than looking, REALLY LOOKING, seeing what there is to see. Little pinpoints, little drill holes. Sucking you in. Knowing what they're doing. Knowing EVERY WORD YOU SAY.

I tried. I gave her a fair chance. Took her out with the rest of us, the whole family so to speak, she had outings, money spent. Not that she appreciated it but she got it all the same. She never relaxed somehow. Difficult, withdrawn. Never said THANK YOU FOR TAKING ME WITH YOU UNCLE FRANK. Never said anything much at all. Never see that in the papers. Clumsy, awkward, a social EMBARRASSMENT. Shyness they called it. They said she was SHY. I lived with it remember, I was there. Nobody else bothered then, nobody else even LOOKED but I DID. If they'd looked they'd

121

have seen but they chose not to. Left it to me. I was the only one who saw what was coming. And I saw all right. I saw it every DAY.

I'm not an unreasonable man.

I argued.

I said to her mother YOU need to do something about it she's YOUR kid SHE NEEDS SEEING TO before things get out of hand. I told her it wouldn't do. LET HER KEEP GOING THE WAY SHE'S HEADED I said and we'll ALL BE SORRY. That STARING all the time like I'd done something wrong. Those silences. They're unnatural in a girl her age, I said, and that WATCHING ME. WATCHING. Like I'd no right to say what was what in my OWN HOME. I said Linda that's how it STARTS how ROT SETS IN. It needs pinching out at source. DUMB INSOLENCE is the WORST KIND, the WORST I said and you're her mother. You just let her DO IT. She has a NEED TO DEFY I said, a need to set you against me, Linda, out of JEALOUSY I said. SPITE. You have to harden your heart for your own good. For HER good. I ONLY HIT HER WHEN SHE'S NAUGHTY I said, it's not SOMETHING I ENJOY. Look I said LOOK at least with me she KNOWS WHAT WILL HAPPEN. If she keeps STARING like that she KNOWS what the CONSEQUENCES WILL BE. She's the oldest I said she ought to be an EXAMPLE. You can't keep on threatening her with something she's not scared of. All right I said. Have it your own way. If you can't I will I said she WON'T EAT with us any more. If she won't learn one way, she'll learn another. She'll COME ROUND QUICK ENOUGH when she's hungry. Go sparing rods and she'll SPOIL. You'll destroy any chance we have of TEACHING HER ANY RESPECT. She'll thank us for it in the end. So I put her in the corner and she went. She knew I meant what I said all right and she went. But it didn't stop. You know what she did? Just stood there. Stood there stock still and WATCHED us eating, WATCHED US, you couldn't think straight, so you couldn't enjoy your food. None of us could. Why SHOULD I turn my back in my own home I said SHE can FACE THE WALL I said but it was just the same. Stubborn. HOURS she could spend, HOURS in the same place staring at the SAME PLACE so you knew she was doing it to get on your NERVES. Don't push me Kimberly, I said. I know what you're doing you don't fool ME. But she pushed. It was in her nature. A NEED TO DEFY. So I put her in the cupboard it was only for an hour or so and it was for ALL OF US I said I AM NOT LOCKING THE DOOR LINDA I said just putting the light off till she sees some SENSE you've got to be cruel to be kind I said but it was still no good. Quiet as a mouse for the first hour or so, the first couple of times then she starts again. She starts WHINING. WHINING. That's what she did. This noise in the cupboard like a collared bitch, getting louder and louder and plainly CALCULATED TO ANNOY. Even when you opened the door you warned her STOP THAT NOW KIMBERLY DO YOU HEAR ME she just kept WHINING pushing her back into the wall, knowing and INVITING IT JUST THE SAME keeping STARING to see if she was HAVING AN EFFECT. I said to her mother I said LINDA she KNOWS what she's doing. I wouldn't put up with that from YOU I said you go giving in to her now and godknows where it'll end. SOMEONE has to mean what they say I said and you starting up won't help all the time this whimpering going on in there, proving something, turning the screw. LINDA I SAID DON'T MAKE ME SHOUT I said. I don't want to have to force you. BUT SHE'LL STAY IN THERE TILL SHE'S SORRY. Somebody HAS TO BE consistent I said KIMBERLY THAT'S YOUR LAST WARNING and she knew I meant it. She knew all right. The whining stopped and I shut the door I said YOU'LL GET OUT WHEN YOU PROVE YOU CAN BE TRUSTED and I went to read my paper. You can't let these things get to you. But the next thing we were in bed when it started the next thing it beggars belief but it's true she started

SCRATCHING I swear with her SCRATCHING DO YOU KNOW WHAT SHE DID? She CLAWED THE CUPBOARD DOOR with her NAILS SHE CLAWED THROUGH TO THE WOOD. Don't tell me that's NORMAL scraping her NAILS on the PAINT till they bled you can't tell me that is NORMAL FOR A SIX-YEAR-OLD CHILD. THEY KNOW THE DIFFERENCE BETWEEN RIGHT AND WRONG. STOP THAT KIMBERLY I said that NOISE like RATS like it followed you to every room in the house I was calm I said STOP THAT KIMBERLY till it was more than FLESH AND BLOOD could stand. JESUSCHRIST LINDA I said it's not even as if she was MINE WHAT MORE AM I EXPECTED TO DO? You switch the tv louder and you still know what for, you still KNOW WHAT SHE'S DOING. So the last night it starts and I said DON'T PUSH ME KIMBERLY down the hall I pressed my mouth to the door I whispered DON'T DO IT PLEASE. I said PLEASE. I begged. And she just KEPT GOING. And that was it.

I put my hand on the doorknob.
I turned the key.

She was sitting next to the hoover. STAND UP KIMBERLY but she didn't. And I hit her NOT hard not to begin with but she just LOOKS not even FLINCHING when you TOLD her what would happen so I did it again STAND UP KIMBERLY curling in a corner NOT EVEN TRYING TO STAND UP just watching while I shook her, I lifted her up put the cigarette onto the skin of the wrist it was MEANT TO BE A LESSON all she needed to do was say she was sorry to STOP not knowing when to STOP the nape of her neck blistering the INSIDE OF HER black mouth open not saying a word just WATCHING while I DON'T TELL ME IT'S NORMAL FOR A CHILD NOT TO CRY OUT.

I SAID TO YOUR MOTHER I SAID SHE'S LET YOU OFF
WITH MURDER. THIS IS ALL YOUR FAULT I said and our
eyes met.

So it was me.

I told her to run the bath but she wouldn't. So I did it.
I filled it with boiling water. I put on the kettle. Someone had to.
Someone had to do something.

I ran the bath. I lifted her up.

Those big blue eyes still staring up like butter

wouldn't

melt

a proper respect

He said her mother would have to know.

There are forms. Forms of consent she has to sign.

His mouth hardly moved.

Bit of a paradox, I suppose. If you went on to have the child and it needed an operation of some kind, you could sign for its treatment. But not for your own. Not for this.

Apart from her in his leather chair, hardening his doctorness like lacquer. It was just how it would be. Her mother would have to know. Alice turned away, knowing the colour of his eyes anyway: the same old scars scratching their way out from under the papers on his desk, familiar stains on the wall rising like continents from the wash of blue. It hadn't used to be that colour. Brown maybe, sage green, but not blue. Nothing light. The ceiling was new too. That tiny wee room up there. It would be full of boxes and godknows again, ladders and no people. No human beings. She could feel it up there now, through the fresh plaster and different paint, pressing down over their shared space like a grudge.

Home.

A cold attic room at the top of the stairs, single-bar heater on all summer.

Home.

There was nothing else on offer for a woman with no job and a wean in tow, a woman who had voluntarily left her man. Mary Quant, permissive age, the pill maybe, but not in Motherwell. Not here. They said he liked a drink right enough but whose man didn't? She'd a hellish tongue on her. If he drank over the odds, he probably needed to: if he'd hit her it would be nothing she hadn't asked for. Jimmy McCardle was all right. Folk had seen him hanging out washing for godsake, so it would be her fault all right and anyway she left him. Her own mother wouldn't have it either. You picked him, she said, putting her mouth that way. It was you wanted the bugger. Anyway, there was no room and she was past the age where she wanted a wean running all over the place. So they went to the doctor's asking for something for the nerves and something for the angina and she had nearly cried when he gave her the prescription, was there nothing he could do? And the doctor gave her a hankie and showed them the upstairs room.

A boxroom store.

Reeking of cardboard, no running water; a thick green curtain on a wire to serve for a door.

A place no-one would knock.

It could be plumbed he said; something, he waved at the doorless gap, something more suitable rigged up. A wash-house, an outside toilet back-to-back with the builder's yard, a tap. He pinked up when she asked how much. It wasn't a question of money, he said. She needn't think of it that way. Some light cleaning duties, the corridors, offices and the surgery to keep things on the right footing, that was all that was needed. Alice remembered looking up, the bulb with no shade. There was nowhere else. Three nights on somebody's livingroom floor, the two of them wrapped in the same blanket and they moved in. Cardboard boxes, a suitcase, the settee and the wardrobe. She carried the trike herself. All the way past the downstairs doors, the bell threatening to bump off the too-narrow stairwell and draw attention to itself, shhh for goodnesssake shhh over and over even though there was nobody else there. He'd said after surgery. He'd been quite clear on that. Her mother's voice saying shh anyway.

There was a lot of that: a lot of keeping quiet and being good. People came Monday to Friday. They waited in a coughing line to clock in with Mrs Beaton in her wee cubicle, the name-badge and the white overall on, signing folk in and giving them tellings off if they were late. They would take the tellings off back with them and sit down, staring at the brown gloss paint till their turn behind the shut door. Sickness, sputum, sniffing weans. Alice kept out the road and played on the drying green, the building-site, the graveyard. If it rained, there was only staying in with the radio too quiet to hear right, looking out the window. A paper shop, a bus queue, a barber's with a stripy pole. She could watch people going in underneath without looking up, came out looking just the same. After five, the big storm door got shut over. You could hear the tumblers all the way up the stairs, know it was ok now. You could come out. By quarter past they'd all be away and the two of them came down instead. It was always dark in the surgery, not just the mahogany and walnut. It felt like somewhere you weren't allowed even when there was nobody else in it. The surgery. The sound of it. The doctor's special doctor place, where people came to be cut into. That was what surgery meant. Not to run, not to shout, not to touch. You knew that somehow from the smell anyway, the stink of bandages and chemical things, the lavender polish her mother put everywhere. You knew it from how things looked, things you couldn't imagine the half about: kidney-shaped metal bowls, empty bottles, black rubber worms in coils on the high shelves, canteens of medical cutlery in leather cases lined in velvet, slim metal probes up to their necks in purple pile. Not to touch. Watching the stuff in case it moved, in case it knew what you were thinking, Alice followed behind her mother's skirt, a rag duster balled tight into one fist. Sometimes, though, the phone would ring and she'd go to answer it. She'd go all the way through to Mrs Beaton's reception bit, leave Alice alone through there with warnings but leave her all the same and the badness would start. It was a terrible thing, the badness in Alice McCardle. It needed watching. Her mother was never done telling her but it didn't get any better. It got worse. In with stuff she'd no business touching like that, it could do terrible things, make her touch things she'd no right to. Left long enough, she'd even reach up for the silver spikes and hooks, the shiny probes in their velvet case. Shafts roughened like files, the glass-smooth tips. One had a mirror in a circle, like something dentists used. You could see yourself in it with the nose too big, face ballooned up and ugly as sin, eyes staring. One sound, one creak of wood under someone's shoe-sole and they'd be back where they belonged so fast not even Alice knew how she'd done it, her face fixed so nothing showed. Not a thing. There had been a mistake only the once, when something had fallen, she couldn't remember what. But she remembered what happened: the brokenness and her mother shouting, her mother crying out of nothing and the crying was the worst. The crying was terrible, the worst thing in the world. Alice hadn't run again, just been careful as hell. She learned how to control her face.

The way she was doing now.

She could see it reflected in the same sickbowls, blurry against the chrome. The black case of instruments wasn't there though. She looked over the doctor's head, back down again. When she turned back, he was looking at her. He had asked her something and now she was making him wait. He sniffed and said it again, clipping the syllables.

I take it you haven't told her?

Alice looked at him. She said nothing.

You haven't told her.

If it had been a question before it wasn't now. Alice didn't know what to say. She was suddenly queasy instead, a cold wave pulsing at the back of her throat. The idea of a breath of fresh air, of going outside, just for a moment. But there would only be the waiting room queue, the bus stop beyond that. Carbon monoxide fumes, the men outside the barber's staring over, then the coming back in. Coming back in. She breathed deep through her nose instead, looked hard at the grey weave of her skirt.

I see, he said. He wrote something on a piece of paper, stared at it looking tired. I see.

No you fucking don't, she thought. But not out loud, never out loud. The fuzz from the light behind his head was making her dizzy, her eyes were starting to nip. Crying was not an option, though. It never had been. Besides she still owed him something: that first appointment with her missing period and kid-on confusion, letting him ask how was her mother keeping and was everything fine at home, letting him work through umpteen stabs at what the trouble was till the joke about gymslip mothers and her face giving it all away. And she hadn't said anything but his smile slipped and he knew anyway. No she wasn't sure she was pregnant but the possibility was what seemed to get him most. It still made her embarrassed thinking about his face, the stiff way it had gone looking at her, letting this something he didn't want to know settle. Four days later, hardly able to hear for ice cream van and weans running home, she called from the kiosk outside the school and he said she better come in again. She knew what it meant, was there with the school tie on before the place shut, polythene bag of books under one arm. He had a lab report on one side of the desk but didn't show it to her, just told her to sit down, told her what she already knew. He looked at a space somewhere between the two of them and spoke to it.

You can't possibly know what this means, of course.

He kept looking at the space. Alice wondered how he knew what it meant, how he could be so sure she didn't but said nothing. Her throat was too tight for saying much anyway. His face got dark. It got redder.

Well, he said. His voice was louder than it had been. Where do we go from here, young lady?

Alice kept her eyes down.

What, for example, do you see as your prospects for you and the child?

Alice tried. She didn't want to have to say anything and irritate him more than she was doing already. But she could make no sense of the question. Child. *Child*. There was nothing she could make it mean. He waited a bit then spoke again, the words *father job marry* coming out his mouth, no more connected than anything else. Till it clicked. He thought she could have it. He seriously seemed to think she could have it.

I can't, she said. I can't do that.

Can't? He looked straight at her. It's a bit late for *can't* now.

Alice sat up in the chair, looked straight back.

No it isn't and I'm not having it. I'm not. I can't.

They were both confused now, taken off guard. The doctor looked at his blotter.

Well, he said. He had other patients waiting. People who had not created problems of their own choosing. People who were genuinely sick. People he would much rather be seeing at this moment. He opened the door without looking at her. It wasn't till she was back in the corridor, listening to the echo of the closing door, her own heels off the gloss walls she felt the dizziness, the damp prickling over the surface of her skin. By the end of the street she had to sit down and doing that the word came to her. Abortion. She wanted an abortion. She walked all the way back to the scheme planning it, making it right: some medical fiction for the few days in hospital, D&C or somesuch. She didn't know what it was but girls her age had them. They were things nobody asked you about so that would be it, over and done with. There would be questions though, him trying to put her off. There were always things you had to prove to doctors. But she would manage. Up the stairwell with the lift not working and the stink of catpiss making her break sweat again, opening and closing a fist in one hand. Whatever it was she had to do or say, she would manage and nobody need be any the wiser. Her mother wouldn't know. Jesus jesus. Alice rested her head on the roughcast at the side of the front door. She could hear the tv on inside, gunshot and sirens. The channel changing, singing. Her mother must never know.

She went for the next appointment with pages of the *Home Medical Companion* learned by heart, could have drawn diagrams of bits she'd never known she'd had before if she'd needed to. He was readier too, though. He did all the asking like it was an exam but that was only to be expected. And she was good at those. School got you trained up for that kind of thing no bother. She was fine, saw everything coming till the last one.

What about school work?

She looked at him. It related to nothing she could think of. There was no way of knowing what he wanted, no time to wonder.

It's fine, she said. I like school. I'm good at it.

He shifted onto something else and told her to come back two days later. A day and a half of still not knowing, feeling for something moving inside that didn't. She kept away from school, walked down by the railway embankments, went home at the usual times to keep in her room. Her mother was pleased. She heard her out the back door, hanging washing. *She's in studying, Isa*, laughter. *Canny complain that way*. Alice kept her head over the book, not reading at all. Back at the doctor's desk, she watched him wash his hands, dry them with a towel. She watched the towel while he sat down, wondering if it had been there before, if her mother had laundered it once. What else she would have to do for this man.

Well, he said. Well. He was looking at her very carefully. We have to make a decision soon.

He took a cloth handkerchief out of his pocket, dabbed his nose, leaned back.

I can't conceal from you this is a very difficult one.

No, she said.

Physically, there's no reason why you shouldn't have a healthy baby. He looked at the hanky, put it back in his pocket. No reason at all.

Thinking about the hanky was making the back of her throat work. She kept her face straight and still, breathing shallow. The doctor clasped his hands, settled deeper into the leather.

But. He arched his eyebrows. We have to think about other things too. You're a bright girl, they tell me. Would you say that's a fair assessment?

Alice said nothing.

The school say you've a chance of good passes later this year. An excellent chance in fact.

She looked at him.

So, he said. So.

Alice kept looking.

You spoke to someone at the school? About my exams?

He looked momentarily confused.

You spoke to someone at Braehead High?

Yes.

Alice looked at him till her eyes hurt. She looked at him till he knew there was something wrong. The hanky reappeared, went back to his nose temporarily. It was filthy.

I sought the advice of another professional person, he said. This isn't the kind of decision a responsible person can —

Who? she said. Who spoke to you?

The tone of her voice was a surprise to them both. Not sure, he waited. Then his voice seemed to be coming from far away.

Young lady, he said. He cleared his throat. You need all the help you can get. The school are prepared to say you should be given a second chance and I am satisfied to take that on trust. And if that doesn't suit you – he shook his head – I'm at a loss to know what you want.

Yes, she said eventually. Thank you. She could hear her breath coming through her nose, short catches. Yes.

He picked up a pen, rustled some papers.

It's not over yet, by any means. We'll need the agreement of the consultant and so on. But things can begin to move forward at least. We can't, after all, afford the time for the kind of social niceties you might prefer.

No.

Something was past now. They were moving on. Alice started rocking gently. Things were going to be all right. When she got out of here, time to think, things were going to be all right.

I'll come with you now, if you like, he said. Get it over with. She'll have to know sooner or later.

She almost smiled at him.

There are forms, he said. Forms of consent. Things she has to sign for the hospital.

It was only then she realised. She realised who he would explain to, where he was proposing to go. As she was meant to. After all, they said she was a bright girl. He could see it in her eyes and the terms were not unreasonable. What if the lassie was sixteen, the signature not necessary? The letter of the law was not the point. He was the doctor. He was an old family friend and the woman ought to know. He held out the forms.

Townhead Road flats is it? The same number?

The same number. The lift not fixed. The smells and those words painted up the stairwell. She couldn't hide any of it. Not a thing. The chair scraped when she stood up. The doctor opened the door.

the bridge

They left the boy with the painted eyes behind and made for the door. She glanced back while they paid at the till, watching to see if he was moving yet but he wasn't. Not so much as an eyebrow. Nineteen, maybe, his hair gelled into oil-slicked feathers, peering through that mess of green eyeliner at the sugary Formica as if his life depended on it. He'd been sitting that way since they came in: through their two coffees and Charlie's brandy, the same slumped shape and fixed stare, the cup beside him untouched. The same way he was now, in fact. Just a wee boy for crying out loud. She heard Charlie opening the door beside her, the sucking sound of seals being broken. He stood holding it, nodding for her to go first, its weight braced against one arm. She flicked her eyes in the boy's direction again, knowing he wouldn't be any different, hoping anyway. Then back to the open door. It wasn't a real choice. You didn't start things you couldn't finish, create expectations and just fuck off. That was the worst thing, the worst thing imaginable. Sometimes you just had to let well alone. She ducked under the waiting arm, telling herself that was just how it was. You had to believe that or you went crazy. Sometimes the only thing you could do was nothing at all.

Outside was cold. That thick dark way it went in the city and freezing. The wind would be coming off the river. He liked it here at night, he'd said: the water, the lights and the skyline. Cmon Fiona, he said, I've been in all day; the fresh air and everything, talking her into it. Then somehow they'd walked for a million miles and ended up at the cafe. They might be going there now, though. His hand swung next to hers as they walked but she didn't reach for it. Only knowing him this short while, it seemed the safest option. The most prudent option. It wasn't the easiest. Even here, walking down this perishing backstreet she could feel it: the wish to touch. Not just to take his hand but to caress him, to run her hands under the leather of his jacket and over his chest, feel his heartbeat warm against her mouth. His perfectly smooth, hairless thighs: the white slither they made moving between hers. Trying to control the thing, to keep walking in a straight line thinking this stuff was making her feel dizzy. Well, that and the fact they'd hardly slept: the ages they'd spent draining the same bottle, repeating the same exchanges about the same people before he'd finally shown her the spare bed; a further age of silences, reluctances to say goodnight and mean it before he'd gotten in beside her. Then, after the sex and the crying – it happened to some women sometimes – waking on and off through what was left of the night to find this other body: those long, pale arms cradling her shoulder, the crisp scent of his neck when she breathed deep. But that wasn't here, in an open place and sober. He was, after all, someone she hardly knew. Meeting every so often because you'd been to the same art school and you were friendly with their sister wasn't the same as knowing somebody. She'd always admired his stuff, written once or twice saying as much, not expecting replies. Then the chance sighting, his shout across the pub on his last visit home, *if you're ever in London* etc. Probably drunk. Probably thinking she'd never take it up. But she had. Now this. This whatever it was. This melting in the gut when she looked at him. This unanticipated, sudden, shocking, lust. On the other hand, maybe it wasn't lust at all. Maybe she was just tired, suffering from weakness of a more banal sort altogether. The pavement had narrowed now, Charlie walking ahead beneath the streetlight. She watched him – the width of him under stretched leather, the pale drift of skin against the collar's edge – feeling an involuntary muscle clench inside. Tired was bugger all to do with it, the muscle said. If he got in beside her tonight, tired was the last thing she'd be thinking about. Tired would wait. If, though. There was certainly an if about the whole business. If if if. Oily stones scuffing her boots, rags of litter. He turned the corner, jacket creaking as he dug his hands into the pockets, and kept walking.

The bridge was there without warning: right there as she turned. Charlie had started up already, his shoes making flat coffin-thumps on the metal plates. Good shoes, decent soles. He hadn't seemed the walking type and neither he was, much. But he needed to get out and about at night, he said: get the paint stink out his nostrils, observe. The railing was bloody freezing. Gloves would have been good but neither of them had any. Godknew how Charlie managed in this weather. He was so fucking thin. She'd had a notion to make him a big pot of soup this afternoon, soup full of barley and rib-sticking things that would last a few days but she hadn't. He didn't seem to need much of a pretext for acting touchy, making out he was being patronised. Katrin called him twisted. On the other hand, it was possible he wouldn't even have noticed the soup, nomatter how much she'd made. He forgot sometimes, his word: forgot to eat. She'd taken him in some rakings out the fridge at lunchtime and he hadn't bothered. She'd eaten both platefuls herself, watching him paint. Three hours without it becoming boring, without conversation, feeling privileged to be there. Maybe feeling she was learning something. Veins like rope on his forearms. She was thinking about Charlie painting, the sexiness of his total absorption, when she almost fell over the man.

None-too-visible but there all right, a man folded into the corner of the platform, legs splayed over the studs of iron sheeting. Fiona could see an open-necked shirt, no socks showing above the rim of canvas shoes, an open cardboard box and a sign with something written on it. I NEED MONEY. The colour of the bridge lights made everything look blue, unwholesome but you could read it if you looked hard. I NEED MONEY. Of course he did. And she'd nearly fallen over him like he was so much rubbish. She had change somewhere, though. Lots of it. Groping in the shoulderbag found two receipts, a postcard, bits of Polo wrapper needing flung away. The man looked up as she riffled for the purse, a glint of eyeball through shadow. Warmth was inching up her neck like creeper, unstoppable. The A-Z, an identity card, godknew what else. Then it dawned on her. She'd left the purse behind at Charlie's place. The man coughed, whispered thank you. Before she had done anything. He was looking at her too, both eyes taking her in. Thank you. Fiona looked back. The accent, the straight stare. It was the same man. A couple of years ago now, but still recognisable. She'd been waiting in what was left of the fog outside the pictures and he'd come out of nowhere, aiming straight for her. She'd thought he was going to ask for the time, was lifting her wrist to tell him till she realised he was keeping coming, till he was far too close for comfort, and he was whispering. I have no money. She remembered standing, the wrist uselessly upturned, a scent of alcohol and some kind of medical stink. Noticing he wasn't wearing a jacket and doing nothing. He'd had to repeat himself, increasing the volume and slowing down as though she was foreign or daft. MONEY. CAN YOU GIVE ME SOME MONEY? English public school vowels throwing her further. She remembered saying Sorry? like a halfwit and him looking, drizzle spangling on the tips of his hair. I. HAVE. NO. MONEY. MONEY. UNDERSTAND? Rubbing his thumb against the next two fingers, feeling empty space before he opened his hand. She had looked at the hand, soft and plump beneath the dirt. A beautiful hand. All she found to fit in it was a couple of small coins and one of them, she saw when she looked again, one of them was Irish. Thank you, he said. Voice up a notch or two, precision sarcasm before he kissed her. He kissed her mouth, made a wet patch that smeared onto her cheek as well, looked hard into her eyes. Thank you very much. And she had stood and let him. Hadn't moved. Refused to meet his gaze but hadn't shifted at all. They must have stood like that some seconds before he went. Just a shadow of him beneath the pillars by the time she was able to move herself, touch the ghost he had left on her face. Now here he was again, angled against the metal girders at her feet. The same queer sense of shame. It was the same man.

From somewhere far away, a light snapping sound. Fiona looked up. On the next level, waiting on the first step of the walkway, Charlie was cracking his knuckles. He was looking down, wondering what was keeping her. Quickly, without having to think about it, she reached for the note in her back pocket, the twenty she'd drawn from the bank machine to tide her over on the journey home tomorrow. It sifted out easily, open and warm. Then, hoping neither man would notice that's what it was, she dropped it in the box. Sorry, she said. Sorry. She ran up the remaining flight still saying it, this time for Charlie. Sorry. Thank god it was dark. Charlie noticed nothing, though. Just gave her one of those half-smiles he did, raised his eyebrows. And walked on.

She reached the top out of breath. Charlie was already staring out over the water, the river beaded with lights.

Look at it, he was saying. Look.

He sounded pleased. Behind him, white neon furred with mist. The view was St Paul's, city blocks, a skyscraper reflecting the water, the odd boat tugging on a rope. Beyond, a slab of indistinguishable shadows threaded with car lights.

London, she said eventually. It looks like London.

He laughed.

Well, it does. She was smiling back now, easier. You tell me what else it looks like then.

He said nothing. They waited side by side, letting the silence sift back. It was ok, this silence. Not chummy exactly but not hostile, just needing to thaw out a bit. She looked at him sideways.

You like living here?

I don't know. He breathed out, the exhalation turning to smoke over his lip. Depends what you mean by *like*.

She shrugged her eyebrows. Just you sound . . . I don't know . . . as though you're admiring something. I thought you sounded fond for a minute.

Ah. He sounded as though he'd just found something and was amused by it. Do I Feel I Belong Here, is that it?

Maybe, she said. I suppose so.

No, he said. The word came out like a silk scarf. Nooooo thank you.

Maybe he just didn't like talking about himself much. Some people didn't.

I'm stuck with Glasgow, she said. Only place I know how to work the buses.

She laughed to let him know it could be a joke if he liked. He didn't.

I like it too, though, she said. Glasgow I mean. When I'm there I take it for granted I suppose but coming back on the train or something, there's a kind of . . . relief. I don't know whether that counts as a sense of belonging but it's there all right.

He looked as though he was listening but didn't speak.

I don't think a sense of belonging is such a bad thing, really. Maybe that's a kind of couthy thing to say, not very sophisticated or cosmopolitan. But I do.

She was talking too much.

So, she said. What about you?

A boat on the far bank was nosing continually in the same direction, sucking grey weed towards itself from the river wall. Charlie said nothing.

What do you think? she said.

No, he said. The sound of his voice was a surprise. No. I can see what's here is nice to look at but it doesn't have anything to do with me really.

His eyes were fixed on something miles away. Fiona tried to see it too, working out what he was talking about. It took her a moment to realise he was still answering the first question. He must have been thinking about it while she was wittering away about Glasgow and only just come up with an answer.

I suppose I feel something for New York because of the Art School, he went on. I did all my growing up there and it kind of . . . kind of sticks you to somewhere. Coming back was − he tailed off, shook his head. Horrible. That's the word. Fucking horrible. But that's finished. I don't have any friends there any more. He looked at her briefly out of the corner of his eye. People I know but not really friends.

You must have somebody, she said.

Katrin had told her he was married out there. There was even something about a wee boy but she couldn't remember all that well. It was all a bit personal and a bit vague to start pushing for answers about that though. Charlie said nothing.

Somebody you write to even, phone now and again?

He shook his head.

The bridge was shoogling, rattling beneath her feet. She hadn't realised trains came by this close. When the noise level was low enough she tried again.

What about back home? D'you not have friends there either?

Home, he said. You mean Scotland? Bloody Greenock for godsake?

He was smiling now, big generous grin, rocking back and forward on the rail and looking down at the water.

Well, you are aren't you? Scottish, I mean.

He snorted, said nothing.

Is it the word you don't like? You don't feel Scottish, is that it? Give me a shout if I'm getting warmer.

He snorted again, keeping her hanging a moment longer.

Well, he said. A long drawl before he warmed up. Well, sometimes. Not often but sometimes. Mostly when other people provoke it though. In the States, for example: they'd ask you stuff, stuff they expected you to know — politics and history, current trends in the Scottish cultural scene kind of thing. Recipes even. I didn't know. He laughed. I didn't care. It was like they couldn't get a handle on that at all. All this banging on about my heritage. *Heritage.* Poor bastards hadn't a clue. Scottish culture jesus christ.

He shook his head in a manner indicative of disbelief.

I used to tell them they'd been misinformed and pretend to be Irish. At least they've got a fucking country. Less embarrassment all round.

Fiona said nothing. His outbreaths were audible in the stillness. When he spoke again, his voice was measured. It was very, very calm.

No. I don't want to belong to any of that thanks. *Being Scottish.* He took a quick swig of air through his nose. At least if you live in London people take you seriously. I don't think I want to belong to anything. Except art maybe, my work.

She could see a stain of paint on his knuckle, a night colour that might be red in sunlight. It might even be blood. Further off, an ambulance was sounding, weaving between unseen buildings.

I know what you mean about Glasgow, though, he said. He laughed. Scared of the big bad world out there. Some folk are uncomfortable anywhere but in a rut, I suppose. It serves a function.

The stained hand clutched the railing, relaxed despite the chill. She watched it for a while then turned her eyes up to his face. He was swaying slightly, a cloud of condensation like an aura round his head.

He looked very young somehow. The skin on his cheeks flushed, his eyes shiny and pink-lidded. Maybe he was trying to wind her up. Maybe he was trying to sound surer than he felt and it just came out that offensive, arrogant way. Maybe he was high on something.

Well, she said, cagey. It seems to suit me.

He smiled again, looking at her now. A generous, sensual smile. She dropped her shoulders a little more.

I wouldn't like to live here anyway.

He said nothing.

It's nice and everything. Not intimidating. London's just a collection of wee towns really. It's all the different bits coming together that is the best thing about here. She breathed in deep. But it can get so . . . well . . .

He cocked his head. So *what*?

It can get awfully . . . cozy, you know. The seat of government, the critical establishment and all that. Just it must be so easy to get . . . sucked into those kind of priorities down here and think it's the world. That they mean something more important than they in fact do.

His smile had gone.

Cmon Charlie, this place can be a helluva rut as well. You don't have to look far. Wee elitist games and who knows who, the right accents, faces fitting. That stupid insider mentality. You know fine what I mean. London isn't the Big World at all. It can be a beautiful place, a seductive place. But it's never struck me as particularly important. It's also as parochial as get out. Don't kid me on you haven't noticed.

I wouldn't know he said, turning away. I don't have the same need to react against it as you obviously do.

React against it? React against what?

What you call the establishment. Insider mentality. I've better things to do with my time than get het up about that stuff. Like paint.

His hand slid off the rail and up inside the jacket cuff.

Establishment. Jesus. Very sixties.

She could see he was frowning and waited, silent, in case she made it worse. Volatility went with talent, they said. Maybe it did. Maybe Charlie was tortured by stuff going on in his brain, great thoughts or something and it made him snappy, volatile. Maybe it was just how it was.

People spend too much time on things that don't matter, he said. Where you belong and stuff. What difference does it make?

He sounded very sure but at least he wasn't huffy. She waited to see if there was more to come.

I got homesick once, he said. The year I did in Berlin. Now my German's pretty good, right? I could understand the sense of humour, the references. I knew most of what was going on but I never talked much. Not with the people from the art school, even other places. They thought it was because I wasn't up to the language, the patois and so on but it wasn't that. I knew it wasn't. I just couldn't be bothered.

The thin metal sheeting was shaking again. Another train.

Do you know what I mean? Just there wasn't anything I had to say about any of that stuff: people's kids, who said what to who, who was having an affair with who, buying furniture and getting a wee place to stay – it was all so . . . I don't know. I just couldn't see what was meant to matter about it all. It was all so bloody ordinary.

The last word swallowed off inside engine noise, the click of resettling wheels. He kept looking at her, the blond hair rimmed with silver from the neon, his eyes with those rings that needed sleep. Inside the sound of the train passing, he looked like his bones would splinter at the slightest pressure, shatter like eggshell. And he didn't know. He didn't know how not well he looked. How child-like.

Maybe that's all there is though? she said. She said it very gently. He looked over, his eyes wide. I mean what's ordinary is what's universal, isn't it? That's where the biggest meanings are.

He kept looking at her.

Aren't they?

Jesuschrist, he said. He laughed. Jesus. If that's true I might as well jump off this fucking thing now.

She wanted to touch him but this was not the moment. She could ask something though, make some kind of contact to stop him digging the trench any deeper. The train was past, silence expanding. It should be now. He beat her to it though, made a kind of laughing sound, air hissing over his teeth. He tilted his neck while he did it, staring into the black sky.

D'you know what I think?

No, she said.

I think. He paused. I think. I think the less time I spend with people the better I like it. People are always a waste of time in the end. They don't think, don't prioritise their fucking lives. People *wear you down*. At least painting makes something. See, my trouble, Fiona, my trouble is I'm too observant. I *see* everything. If I didn't order some of it on canvas, I'd go round the bend. Art *makes sense*: people *don't*. And I know what I'd rather spend my time on. Any day. Any day.

Neither of them said anything for a moment. She looked out at the skyline, trying not to feel whatever it was that was hurting her chest. Anger, maybe. Whatever it was it was getting bigger.

Too fucking observant, he said again. People like you don't know how lucky they are.

Look, she said. She said it very slowly. I don't think *sense* attaches to anything intrinsically. But you can't seriously be telling me people don't matter.

He said nothing.

Cmon. You're saying for real that people aren't worth anything?

Nothing.

Ok. This supposed Life and Art debate: this notion you're somehow above *ordinary* living order to be an Artist and Life is for the lower orders or something – it's all crap. Maybe male crap, maybe just elitist crap but definitely crap.

He was smiling now, still not looking at her. She didn't know whether she was saying something funny or he was trying to annoy her.

It's worse than crap, it's a con trick, Charlie. If there's no Life there is no bloody Art is there?

And what's Life then? he said.

Talking and interchanging, the raising of weans. Getting by. Behaving decently towards other people. Love, I suppose. If you don't attend to that, you attend to nothing. Love, Charlie.

My god what was wrong with her? This monologue and that word suddenly coming out. She shouldn't have used it, not used a word like that. Not to Katrin's big brother, to someone who could paint the way he could. Not to Charlie. She had to slow down, care less. Try for lightness.

If there's no Life there's no Art. Discuss.

He didn't laugh. Just looked at her, his face blank. It was terrible not being able to embrace him though, make sure things were all right. His hand still lying there on the metal rail, nails flecked. A man who forgot to eat. A man who had kissed her awake.

Was it a mistake coming away from the States then?

Her voice had gone that soft way, like a psychiatrist. A doctor in a film.

He shrugged. I don't miss anywhere. A place is just a place.

The disappointment was unexpected. But unmistakable. It wasn't till she felt it stuck in her chest like cold pudding she knew what she'd been doing. All this time. She'd been wanting him to say something else. A question, maybe, something that wondered what *she* cared about, her work or something. Only he'd never seen her pictures, never asked her to send any when she'd offered. And anyway that wasn't really it at all. What she'd really been wanting was more humiliating still. Some kind of sign, something as trivial as a compliment. An invitation for tonight, that's what she wanted: some kind of possibility opening up between them. She flicked her eyes up to see if he knew somehow. He was hunting for something in the inside pocket, oblivious.

I suppose I don't feel I belong anywhere either, she said.

It was impressively matter-of-fact.

Not till something gets me angry.

He was smiling properly now, feeling better for just having found whatever it was he'd been after. It was fags. A packet of fags.

Unreconstructed Romantic, eh?

She watched the smile widen, his hand slip into the trouser pocket, looking for matches.

You need to pick your fights, Fiona. Look after number one a bit more. Too bloody soft, that's your trouble. You're too bloody serious about the wrong things. You mind Alison Sime? She could paint. She could really paint. You know what she's doing now?

Fiona looked at him, the packet he'd unearthed secure in one hand.

Two kids and the glory of motherhood, that's what she's fucking doing. Not painting. Not bloody making a name for herself. Women's priorities. He shook his head. The things they do to themselves. That's where women always fuck up, you know? Sentimentality. What your lot need to do is realign your priorities.

She knew it wasn't really him. Even while it was happening, she knew it wasn't him that was making her feel so terrible. It was her. If she hadn't got him so riled up, hadn't pressed all the wrong buttons, he wouldn't be saying any of this. Everything was in jeopardy and it was her fault. Even knowing, she hung back, reluctant to acknowledge the fact it wasn't coming right, that saying anything else was just going to make it worse.

So, he said. Here endeth the lesson. Will we get going?

He had lit up, the thing glued to his lower lip as he spoke. He couldn't understand what was keeping her standing at the railing. They moved together, without touching. They drew close at the top of the steps and without thinking, she asked for a kiss. His proximity made it seem natural. He said No. Just one word. No.

A piece of scarf, a rag of cloth was tied to the rail on the way down but the man was gone. No man, no box, no wee sign. Charlie didn't seem to notice. Fiona looked out over the scrub at the side of the bridge but there was no sign.

Know something, Charlie said. He was buoyant when they got to the bottom. I meant to say when you were doing your mile about Scotland and belonging. Your name, Fiona, it's not Scottish. It's not even old. P. G. Wodehouse or somebody made it up. He raised one eyebrow. And you're telling me about con tricks eh?

He laughed all the way to the tube station.

After the waterside, the tunnel light was harsh and yellow. They avoided looking at each other on the way through. By the time they reached the ticket machines he had become restless, less self-contained. He muttered something about wanting to explain, nothing more. The explanation, whatever it referred to, didn't surface. They sat with one empty seat between them on the tube back, not talking. Soon they'd be back at the house. Maybe it would all be sorted out there: something simple would be said and the tension would lift. Or break. Whatever it was tension did. Maybe the whole thing tonight was a misunderstanding, a nonsense they'd laugh about later. Maybe it was PMT or something. Godknew. The train shivered round a corner and into another station that wasn't theirs. He was playing with the cigarette carton, eyes shut, miles away. She stared at the route map, its circles and interconnecting lines. Another three stops to go. There was an off-licence on the way back, the corner just before his place. She could go in and buy a bottle of something, a bottle of something usually helped. They'd get in and Charlie would fetch the gas heater, make them both something warm to drink. They might sit on the big double mattress on the floor to drink it, move close. Closer. Just three more stops. Further down the carriage, a drunk was trying to stand, preparing to come in their direction. Soon, she hoped, maybe very soon this cold feeling in her chest would go away.

tourists from the south arrive
in the independent state

They touched down four hours late and the luggage hadn't arrived but they didn't mind. These things happened. Even in the most sophisticated of places, these things happened. They spent the time they might otherwise have spent minding in a cluster at the carousel, willing it to start, nodding to clusters of Islanders left over from internal flights. Trying not to stare overmuch, the sight of decent wool knitted into such awful jerseys. They chose instead to listen, feeding their ears on those thick, near-Slavic vowels, now and again, an almost-familiar word crunching with consonants. There was a distinct Eastern Bloc snubness of pronunciation when you attended carefully, really something less harsh than one had been led to believe. Only there was no Eastern Bloc now. No Cold War. The way of the modern world, the forgings of proud independences etc. It was best to welcome it all as a Good Thing. They looked up keen then, prepared to smile their warmest smiles for these people from a colder, possibly even nobler, climate. Odd that their countries being formally separate now should make them feel so much closer, so much more tolerant. Smiles were the least they could do to salute the fact.

The Islanders weren't looking. They had huddled together, lighting a single cigarette and passing it on. They did not smile back. They didn't even notice. And that was perfectly all right too. Of course it was. Gauche to force contact in any case, patronising. They were a people whose history had led them to be wary and rightly so, rightly so. The red-head closest shouted something and gestured with his hands. He had the richest accent. They listened carefully, relishing cadences they recognised from tv documentaries, the odd series. *Taggart, Para Handy.* Catching themselves whispering sample phrases for the feel of it in their own mouths, they almost blushed.

A noise like an industrial crusher sounded suddenly close, making some of the group start. The indigenous group didn't flinch or even turn round. Perhaps they knew it was only the carousel. A first battered carpet bag was already coming through, string and bits of insulating tape binding a rip on the material. Someone who had not plumped for new cases after all. It went round unclaimed. Though they kept their eyes on the luggage vent, nothing more appeared. Not yet. Not for a while perhaps. The Islanders had begun passing round oatcakes and a page of a concertinaed newspaper. Racing Tips. So unperturbed they were laughing. They waited coughing, riffling in pockets for things that weren't there. Some wandered to the pinboards inexpertly attached to the walls, the single poster left intact with its patterning of trees and water. Lock Lomond perhaps. Lock Ness. One torn banner had nothing left but its words: THE BEAUTIES OF ROYAL DEESIDE against a ripped edge. An irony, perhaps, a joke. The conveyor kept turning with nothing on the belt.

When they looked back, something was missing. It took a moment to register: the Islanders had gone. Four douts, one of them still smoking on the tweed-coloured tile, and an empty IRN BRU bottle were all that remained. The luggage had arrived. Whatever the Islanders had had to collect was gone, leaving the tourgroup's flight bags and cases, the odd rucksack piled in a crumbling mountain behind the only trolley. They had no sooner begun to gather them together when someone appeared, a shout and an arm waving from the double glass door. THE BEAUTIES OF ROYAL DEESIDE slid past for the last time as they walked into the clear night air.

Outside smelt of faulty incinerators and fish suppers. A faint undertone of malt. The arm that had waved belonged to a thin man in shiny trousers and no jacket despite the cold. They noted he had not shaved either but he smiled and pointed to a bus half-mounted on the paved area. An old bus. He kept pointing till they made for the single step up onto the platform, helping the heavier among their number inside where the seats were pleasingly whole and covered with tartan flocking despite the strong tang of nicotine and spilled alcohol. Still, everything seemed very clean. They were sure it was all very clean. They were still settling when the bus started without warning, elbowing heavily onto the road, and the interior lights switched off. Some thought about asking to have them switched on again then thought not. It might have showed a terrible lack of something, lack of awareness of the need to conserve energy. In any case, the driver had put the radio on: something jolly on an accordion. And with the lights off it was possible to see the wide streets much more clearly. Wide streets and long stretches of wasteground. They noted a pile of rubble that might well have been something impressive once, something important. Then more wasteground. Eventually, the streetlamps came into view. By their light, hoardings with unreadable exhortations became visible, graffiti under the bridges. Doubtless the work of dissidents, though whether of dissidents before or after recent events would be impossible to say. The driver's high nasal whine joined in the radio-singing only he was talking. They did not recognise the words but he was pointing at something, possibly a landmark of national significance. They peered out of the windows, rubbing holes in the condensation already gathering there, saw nothing but late-night neon, a stretch of warehouses closed for the night behind shutters. A flyover spanning a shimmer that might have been water.

On the other side, streets broad and lonely as ship canals stretching to the edge of the sky.

When the bus finally tipped them out at a too-big hotel, it was snowing. They fetched their own things from the belly of the bus because the driver did not, nodding to reassure there was no assumption he was at fault. They had hesitated only to be sure, aware of the fine line. They walked inside then, cold and getting colder over the thinning Black Watch shag pile to a high reception desk. Behind it, three women wearing suits and 2 am faces waited under clammy electric light. The sign on the counter, PASSPORTS MUST BE SURRENDERED ON RECEIPT OF KEYS NO TICK, made them uneasy but they did not quibble. They were tired. Zips fizzed cautiously, careful not to break the quiet; they booted baggage through the dust drifts towards the desks. The passports were new, a different colour and awkward to find. Somewhere to the right, the sound of football on tv veered blurrily close then swallowed off again. The women waited patiently, sucking dark lips. Still foraging, they tried smiles but did not hold them long. It was better to keep eyes on the reflections of their own shoes on the dull tile, the mosaics on the far wall. Blue with white webbing.

The river Clyde, the wonderful Clyde.

The woman behind the counter had sung it. She stopped, took the passport.

The Clyde, she said. You'll have seen it on the way from the airport.

A passable Standard English except for the phrasing. Behind her, representational water flowed down the wall in tiny squares while she looked from passport photo to face and back again, her mouth tightening at the corner in an attitude that resembled amusement. They tried to think that was not so. It would just be tiredness playing

162

tricks, the mild paranoia of new places striking home. And they were indeed. They were very tired.

Now they held pink hotel cards, keys. Behind a square-edged pillar, the LIFT sign, handwritten, appeared. Something to walk towards. They shuffled inside, six at a time, watched the red numbers on the way up, left without speaking. They wanted only to find their respective rooms. Alone and quickly, tiptoeing past the sleeping janitor in his den, they pursued the numbers on their keys. None knew when breakfast would be served, or where. No-one had offered or said. Those who had learned any prior to the trip had not used their patois. They did not want to start now. Without help, they found the right doors but the locks were resistant, reluctant to give in. They persisted, they muddled on, twisting their wrists and fingers in the hope that the next turn would be all it took. But now, fifteen floors high in the New Independence Hotel, glimmers of admission that things were not all they had hoped for were undeniable. They slumped then, leaned against the cool walls, gathered strength. They tried not to think about the possible quality of guest soap or toilet paper, whether the curtains would close. The inevitability of a monster tv in one corner. That the sound of bagpipes and that single word shouted from streets distant would not go away. It was impossible not to sigh.

Yet behind the closed eyelids, they hoped for better things. Perhaps the door would surrender next try: the room that opened before them might be cheerful, modest and clean. They would walk inside, close the old day out, leave luggage where it fell and tumble onto the freshly-turned sheets. The Kelman novels they had brought for atmosphere would wait or be used, spines cracked open, to place over weary faces to keep out the morning light. When it came. And it would. It would certainly come. Morning always did.

The shout again, the same expletive. A sound like an owl.

Hooch.

Hooch.

But for now they were still in the corridor, keys hard inside their fists, yet to comply. They heard others in adjoining corridors sigh too, the thud of shoes against unyielding wood. It was three am. And they thought how understanding they had wanted to be.

How generous. How tolerant.

How kind.

he dreams of pleasing his mother

The blue dress flickers like a cold flame.

She was walking along the edge of the road, one foot dragging a little but her pace even, without hesitation. Making for the truck. The truck was the biggest thing apart from the sky: vast red body buffed hard as mirror, radiator gills burning like magnesium flashes. Dazzling. The sun must be high, up there. It had to be though he couldn't feel it. If he looked carefully there was heat-haze, wavy lines moving over the solid machine up ahead, making it ripple, but no warmth or sound, no rush of air on his cheek. Maybe he was behind glass. He looked without moving his head, casting his eyes side to side whilst keeping his body rigid but it was impossible to tell; not without stretching out a hand and giving himself away. To show any form of fear would be self-defeating. There was no room for wrong moves. Even though there was no-one else, no-one else visible anyway, you couldn't be too careful. People were surprising. And there was always the possibility of being watched from control boxes, the whole road being monitored by cameras. She was still there, coming steadily down the kerb. He screwed up his eyes, peering to see her face, read it for clues of some kind. She was still too far away. He realised then he had been wondering if she knew anything he didn't, if she had even set this up somehow. Terrible thing to think about your own mother but that was what he did sometimes, the kind of bad bastard he was. He kept watching her all the same. She seemed no closer but things were clearer somehow. He could tell things he hadn't been able to before. The dress, for example. It wasn't a dress. It was a two-piece: one of those skirt and cardigan affairs she liked with a string of black beads. His mother did not own black beads, they weren't the kind of thing she wore, but there they were, double-looped on her chest. Maybe they were new, a present from someone. It would please her if he noticed them and made some remark. Even at this distance he could tell she was smiling, giving him a hint. A big smile. So big it made her teeth look longer, whiter. Almost unnatural. The skin on the back of his neck bristled. Maybe they weren't her teeth at all. They could be false, capped maybe. Or. He felt dizzy thinking about the or but he was thinking it anyway. Or they were the teeth of some other animal entirely. He looked at it hard, knowing even as he did it there would be no way to tell. Because if it was a beast, if it really was some terrible thing with terrible powers the likes of which he could only begin to guess at, it would have done the disguise properly. Dear god dear god. The need to struggle to remember to give nothing away, to remember not to run. He warned himself against being a child and a fool several times, keeping his face impassive. It helped to remember the pain in his head was not visible and the rest of his face was good at obeying orders. If he had learned nothing else, he had learned that. Eyes refocusing, forcing his brow smooth. Now he'd pulled himself together, she looked fine. The smile was perfectly normal. He toyed briefly with the idea of smiling back, rejected it. If it looked forced or too eager, wrong somehow, it would ruin things. Whatever happened, he knew he better not mention the animal idea, not even as a joke. Shame caught his chest just thinking about it. If she knew what he'd been thinking, if she knew what went on in his head, if she even suspected. The shame pressed harder. And she would, all right. She'd notice. She noticed fucking everything. But things were ok now. They were under control. She hadn't shown any displeasure so far, hadn't really shown any sign she'd seen him at all. That being the case, it was entirely possible he was invisible and all this worry was for nothing. Maybe that was it. Maybe he just wasn't there. Cheered, he turned his head up, let his shoulders relax. The sudden fear invisibility could be construed a major fault occurred and was pushed away. No need to get paranoid.

She stopped walking then.
Level with the red cab, she stopped walking.

She waited a moment, brushing the skirt sleek with one hand, preparing and he could not help but feel a flush of pride. Mother. She always liked to look neat. She looked up at the cab and reached for the handle, stretching. One foot rose to the black platform and he saw she was wearing her best shoes, the ones with ankle straps and the little cuban heels. He concentrated on watching the shoes in case her skirt rode up when she hauled herself onto the step. That would feel unpleasant, voyeuristic. He looked hard at her foot. The foot was so clear he was sure the face would be too and he was right. Mother's face. She was wearing a touch of powder and lipstick and looking into the cab interior with something approaching delight. It was definitely her though. He watched her steady herself then launch upwards, the familiar head and blue two-piece cramming themselves into the cab, the mouth-parts of that great red beast perched on the road ahead. When she reappeared, high off the ground behind the windscreen, she looked smaller somehow. Like a woman he didn't know. He wondered if he should shout, give her some kind of warning he was here after all. Then her features creased, the smile returning, and he knew his warning was not something she needed at all. She was perfectly fine. Putting on her crash-helmet, a bullet-shaped dome with a full-face shield. She didn't need him for a thing.

He watches the woman he knows to be his mother vanish behind the polarised visor, her fingers secure the clip at the neck. Her ring finger glitters before it drops out of sight. He knows that ring. The mark she made on his face when he was six is still there, a light score. That was an accident, though. She always said it was an accident. That ring doesn't come off. They will need to bury her in it, he thinks. No-one will ever see it again. His nose is running now but her hands offer nothing. They are still out of sight. They are out of sight because she is turning the ignition. The sides of the truck quiver. Exhaust fumes cloud the chromium sheen of the radiator muzzle but he hears nothing. Even when he puts out his hand, there is no glass. No bars, nothing. He really must be here. He must.

When he looks down he sees feet. They are wearing his shoes. Half on the grass verge, half on the surface of this road that might be a motorway though he has seen no evidence, no other cars. Maybe they would still come. The vibration he could feel, the trembling, had to be caused by something. His feet – they can be no-one else's – stand on tarmac and earth. There are no flowers between the green blades. When he begins to walk – it is the only thing he can think of to do – the shoes stay put. Of course they do. The clothes are only trappings. It is him she is here for. Keeping his expression still, measured, as though he knew all along, he walks carefully over the cold asphalt in his stocking soles. He is dimly aware he does not want to do this but tries not to notice. Stray stones and shale, step after step, he just keeps going to the white centre-line. He stops. There is a hole in the sock-tip, a rag-nail poking through. Noticing chills him. It chills him hollow. It reminds him he cannot put off knowing what will happen now. He stares at this sign of his body's existence, his knuckles whitening. Then looks up.

The juggernaut grins.
Coming and going like a red mirage, settled on its hunkers.

The scarlet and silver casing, the deep, black treads.

He lifts his head then, the whole heavy weight of it, levelling his eyes to show he is not afraid. The juggernaut sighs, releasing brakes. She would be doing that. Her hand. And now they will be resettling on the wheel because the tyres are beginning, rolling slowly forward. He swallows, wondering if she can see him yet, if there is a chance he will be able to make her look directly at him. Maybe when she is closer he might even be able to make her hear. The new beads. If he has time to mention them, say how nice they look. She might smile then. She might even reach for the brakes. His throat is dry. A vein in his neck is pumping blood. It keeps doing it.

Ahead, in the thick, still air of this place he does not know yet has been all his life, the truck is growing larger. He flicks his eyes to the road behind, hearing the other cars, other engine sounds growing louder. They might well reach him before she does. The curve of a bonnet perhaps at hip-height: whether metal or rubber will make contact first. He has no way of knowing how much it will hurt. But he knows he will not move. Not now. He would just wait here till she came: nomatter what condition he was in when she arrived, he'd be here. To see if this time it would be different. He wanted to see if he could provoke compassion. But even if he couldn't. Even if she didn't look or acknowledge him at all before the wheels bore down, he wanted to know he'd given it his best shot.

He tilted his chin, catching the last of the sun. He had good bone-structure. And he very much wanted to be beautiful. For her to be proud. Beautiful, deliberate, dignified, he waited for his mother.

last thing

we were
coming

coming back from the pictures with half a packet of sweeties still
coming round the corner at the Meadowside with Mary saying she
was feart to go up the road herself Mary is feart for everything but so I
said I'll take you because I'm bigger than her the film thing we'd saw at
the pictures that Halloween thing wasny really scary I don't think but
Mary saying she hated all the screaming the big knife was horrible one
time her brother pushed one under the toilet door she said and told her
to slit her wrists but he's not right Billy he works a place they make
baskets or something he's not right in the head so I said I'll take you up
the road offering her a sweetie it got stuck to the back of her teeth and
she was laughing kidding on her mouth was glued shut and she
couldn't talk only make these moaning noises because her mouth was
all stuck together when this shape a big kind of shadow thing started it
came out of the close at the corner of the main street right where the
streetlight is at the corner a big shape coming out and turning into a
man he was only a wee bit bigger than Mary so maybe he was a boy
really and he said
     I've lost my mate
     just like that he said and away back in again away in the close he
had come out I just looked but I couldn't see him but he was definitely

175

there you could hear him saying it again in there I've lost my mate only a wee thin voice with no body now but you couldn't see maybe he was round the back garden or something and I thought he must be lost too the man maybe not from here with him speaking funny the way he did not knowing you didn't wander about in people's gardens this terrible idea of being lost and maybe not knowing where you were and not being able to find the person who had come with you like losing the only thing you understood and I went in Mary was kind of hanging back she didn't like people she's an awful feart kind of person Mary she gets rows from her mother for talking to folk she gets rows for just being there but I went in away after the sound of the voice that had lost its friend and was maybe lonely I went in after the voice and I couldn't see him at first it was too dark too

dark off the main road and I didn't like it was too dark I couldn't hear anything any

more and I was nearly shouting for Mary to come too it was frightening expecting to go in and help somebody and suddenly they weren't there to be helped and it was like a dark tunnel between nothing and where she was out there so I was about to shout her when something

some thing wrapped it

self around my neck I didn't know just felt the tilt backwards and couldn't work out why I was unsteady on my feet till the thing went tight in my neck like a piece of pipe or something it was blocked a stuck thing poking into where I needed to breathe and my legs going soft like they wouldn't be able to hold me up I just went like a dolly because I got a surprise not knowing what it was till I was being dragged backwards back

wards away from the road the streetlight out there the yellowness kind of slipping further away because somebody some body was dragging me by the neck a man he said YOU'RE COMING WITH ME but his voice wasn't right like he was choking

or crying maybe something was wrong it was definitely the man saying
YOU'RE COMING WITH ME and he shoved one of his hands up
under my jersey I could feel the big shape of his hand sort of pulling my
jersey under my jacket and going up onto my belly and it made me
stop and breathe wrong it was so unexpected his hand there then he
pushed me round the edge out the close altogether against the wall so
then I could feel the wall being crumbly thon way plaster goes after
years with the wee bits of moss growing through it crumbling through
to the grey stuff underneath you think it would have felt scratchy but it
wasn't it was just this stuff disintegrating under where he was pushing
me back against the wall so it was hard to keep breathing right with his
hand pushing under my chin so all I could see was the sky a funny
colour with the orange off the streetlight making wee grains in it like
off milk but right then right that minute something kind of turned in
my head something kind of clicked and I wanted to look him right in
the eye

it was what I really wanted to do I wanted to
just see his face just
look him in the eye he was pushing my face so hard my nose was
running he was hurting my wrists but I kind of pushed my head
straight till I could see because I wanted to see his face I wanted to stare
at him he was cutting off where I was trying to breathe and know I just
wanted him to know to see me and know what he was doing the noise
of Mary greeting from the street out there I could hear her in the place
by the close mouth Mary a terrible coward and not even sure where I
lived and even if she found it I was scared she got a row so would I for
being out I could get a row easy for there being marks on my neck
maybe hit I wondered if it looked like lovebites or hit for not being
back on time the face of the man rising a single eye in enough light to
glisten seeing me watching him and thinking it will make a difference
if he can see me so I looked at him

right into his eyes I looked right at him
keeping
    my sights

    clear

    and

still

not flu

A whisper. Peter's voice, muffled through the layer of hollowfill, a word in the unknown tongue. Bloody Dutch.

Rachel peeled her face out the pillow, turning towards more light than was bearable. A magnesium flare on the dressing table mirror. He'd opened the curtains again. The duvet was too close, one stiff corner shoving against her lip. She shifted to avoid it, making one hand an eyeshade against the closed lids. It didn't help much. Tiny silver-red beams, cloud linings the colour of fresh blood, filtered through the spaces between her fingers, the tang of overnight sweat from her open palm nipping the soft-boiled whites till they watered. Bloodshot. That was how they felt: covered with tiny red threadveins. All burst. The sounds were still going on in the other room. She could hear them quite distinctly: a polythene bag opening and closing, taking surreptitious ages, then muttering. She listened hard but the words were indecipherable. Not understanding didn't mean they didn't filter through, though. The two of them thinking they were being so careful, thoughtful, trying not to wake her up. Lying like this magnified things, made them impossible to blank out. Even so, she knew fine she ought not to be doing it. Listening to folk behind their backs. Eavesdropping, they called it. Well, that's what Enid Blyton books called it. She couldn't think of any other word. Eavesdropping. Bloody disgraceful. Rachel closed her eyes again, shifting the hand that had covered them over an ear instead, trying to behave. The other hand had surfaced from beneath the sheet, she used it to rub a sore place just behind the hairline. The roots there thick, greasy. Needing washed. One eye opened, found the clock. Five to five. It was always five to five. Over a week now and she still hadn't replaced the fucking batteries. Rachel moaned, moved to sink her face into the pillow again when another sound made her stop short. Knife noise, the scrape of stainless steel off cheap china. Her cups, her knives being passed hand to male hand in the kitchen. The bastards were making breakfast.

The flash of anger caught her by surprise. Unpleasant surprise. Rachel opened her eyes, making them water. The man was a guest for heavensake, a foreign guest. He was here because he'd been asked, because he'd been invited. It was her had asked him. He was simply making his breakfast, doing as he was told and making himself at home and there was nothing wrong with that. Nothing wrong with speaking Dutch, either – what else was he supposed to speak? It was meant to be the point. Peter's other language. It was for Peter. English didn't feel right in his mouth any more, he said. After eight years in another country no wonder. That beautiful, choked way he spoke, accent so overlaid with the different tongue it was hard to tell where he belonged. Edinburgh born and bred and that silly cow in the delicatessen over the road thought he was South African. Sud Afrique? he'd asked one day, twisting the pitch up on the last syllable like a parrot. He'd said it every time since. It drove Rachel cuckoo but Peter just laughed. He was never out that shop. Other ways, though, other ways he just wasn't settling back at all. He fretted about his Dutch going to waste, his pass-for-the-real-thing idioms rusting. So it was *her* that said it, her idea: ask one of your mates over, it's your place too now and he smiled that way that made her stomach slide like sand. A carnal sensation. Less than a week after, when he said Marc was coming, the feeling came again only this time closer to the lower intestine. Someone she didn't know would be sharing their living space for a fortnight. More food and electricity, having to put a camp bed up in the living room every night, whether he would leave his stuff lying all over the place, whether it was rude or bourgeois to care. And Dutch christ christ Dutch. Peter just smiled when she said she was scared. Once. Then he'd gone back to his blueprints, his notes in the margins. There was no-one to blame but herself, after all.

By the time they were standing at the airport, though, clutching bunches of tulips she wasn't sure weren't a joke, it seemed better. It seemed better because of Peter's face. She'd never seen him look so something. Radiant, maybe. Happy. Helping to look for someone she'd seen only one bad photo of; relieved, for some reason, when he looked less like Peter than she'd expected. Even if she had made an idiot of herself blocking a whole planeload of folk trying to get by, even if she had felt surplus to requirements, it didn't matter. Watching Peter exchange kisses with the other man, seeing his pleasure, made the apprehensions petty and mean-minded. When Peter gathered her in too, making a three-sided embrace, she knew it for sure. Nomatter what the guy was like. Marc. Nomatter what Marc was like. Everything would be just fine.

Laughter.

Rachel's back stiffened, her ears pricking. In the other room, the toaster popped, ejecting both barrels: a single word emerging from a blur of giggles. There was no other word for it, they were giggling. Her eyes were closing again, one hand rising to her temple. She pressed the warm skin there, feeling the skull beneath push back. Bone under flesh, resisting like eggshell.

It must have been 4, something like 4 am. She had woken with his breath in her ear. A half voice, not making words she could turn into meanings yet. Peter saying something. I don't know what to do. She had thought it an intimacy, the depth of dark and the heavy scent of him next to her, maybe a tenderness, and she had turned, expecting the weight of his hand to fall on her breast. A kiss, perhaps. Her nipples had tensed, waiting. But he didn't reach. He didn't touch her at all. The sheets were cold, he said. He whispered. The sheets were cold. And she had fumbled her hand towards him, finding something cloying, clammy. The sheet on his side damp enough almost to be called wet. Something was wrong. It was not an embrace at all. I don't know what to do, he said. There was a moment of nothing before he repeated it. He didn't know what to do. It was happening again.

Thinking about moving jesus trying to open her eyes. The air inside the room thick as raw meat. Just breathing it in was an effort. She heard him sigh again, the sound vast in the stale blackness. She should have forced him to take those bloody vitamin things. He'd not liked her going on about them but she should have forced him all the same. Now here it was again, another night of this broken sleep and sweating. Four nights in a row. Not ordinary sweating either but rivers of the bloody stuff, his skin in spate. She dragged her hand back from the sheet and lifted her head. Christ, the dizziness, a kind of spiralling soreness behind the eye sockets. It got worse as she hauled into a sit then pushed off the mattress to stand. The blackout curtains left no light to see by, none at all. She found the door anyway, banging her shin on something hard, not able to keep her eyes open for longer than seconds at a time. But she had to do something. The least she could do was get him some clean sheets.

The hall was cooler, the press door opened first tug. The two sheets she expected to see were right at the front, the smell of that fabric stuff rising from traps in the fibres. A smell like peaches, almost soothing. She'd put stuff in the machine specially. They weren't ironed but they were fresh. She bundled them in her arms like a child and went back through. This time the bedside light was on, Peter was standing up. Trying to stand up anyway. She could see him, through half-shut lids and a mesh of eyelash, pulling something on over his chest, tugging it down, hardly able to keep his balance for heavensake. She dropped the clean linen without saying anything and peeled back the duvet ready to dismantle the damp mess underneath. It wasn't easy. She'd made the thing up too fussy: hospital corners, wee games of nursemaid. Now it was a bastard to pull apart. He was suddenly beside her then, reaching to help, blue veins visible through one ghostly wrist. She squinted sideways but there was no comfort in it. He looked exactly the same as the other nights. Terrible. Eyes heavy and skin taut over the high cheekbones, his lips chalked out. He shouldn't be trying to do this. He shouldn't be standing up, never mind anything else. But she said nothing. Trying to tell him how to look after himself always caused more problems than it was worth. It was virtually done anyway. She let him tug the last bit free and dump it with the other castoff already on the carpet. The undersheet was stained and damp too, she touched it to make sure. He caught her eye and they stripped it away, all without speaking. Three sheets to take through to the washing pile. Peter didn't sit down though. He just kept standing looking at her. It wasn't till Peter sighed again that Rachel realised it wasn't the tired kind of sighing at all but another kind that had something to do with her and looked down. She was naked. Hauling the bed apart like a thing possessed and stark, seal-belly naked.

I've no dressing gown.

It hung there, not explaining anything. She wasn't sure why she said it, why it sounded so much like apology. She often slept naked, at least often in summer. Other times when there was a likelihood of sex. A wish for sex. And this wasn't summer. A confused embarrassment was spreading over her skin, some kind of shame she couldn't place. From the corner of an eye, she caught a glimpse of herself in the mirror, a lump of marbled lard. His bathrobe was here somewhere:

she'd seen it in a heap on the floor before she had put the light out. It was still there now she looked, behind the wicker chair leg. She stooped to pick it up, trying not to wonder whether it was right side out, whether he would mind. Whether it was even sanitary: it was probably hoaching with his flu germs, bacteria and microbes and godknows. It didn't matter though. It didn't matter a damn. She wanted to cover herself up before he sighed again, before she did anything else. She shouldn't be barging about naked with a strange man in the house. Not that Marc looked at her much but that was beside the point. Other people's sensitivities and so on: it might have offended him to hell. The belt was in a knot now, a solid knot. When she looked back up, Peter was angled against the bedside, exactly where she had left him. Shaking. His whole body shaking, the clean tee-shirt he'd put on already patched with dark under the arms.

Jesus Peter. Are you ok?

He said nothing.

Put the heater on or something. Sit in front of the heater and get warm a minute.

He didn't look at her but crouched down on his hunkers, reaching for the socket. Rachel watched him feel for the switch, press it once, his neck sheeny with drying sweat. There wasn't a damn thing she could usefully do. Except maybe make up the bed again, hope they both got some sleep, wait for the thing to pass off. Maybe that was all it needed: a decent night's kip and they'd be fine. She turned away from the sound of the fan, the soft billowing of overheated air, heading back to the press for the third sheet.

The shelves were empty. Nearly empty. Just a torn thing like a sleeping bag liner crushed at the back. It was all there was, though. This morning's wash was still up on the pulley: there was no point even checking it. She lifted the torn sheet and went back through not looking. That was what did it. She knew even before the pain registered, a dry sharpness shooting from the ankle, she knew it was her own fault. If she hadn't been rushing, preoccupied, whatever it was she was being. But she had. Her shin and the bedside cabinet collided again, the same shin, the same place. The kind of pain that got worse after initial impact.

Jesus she said. Jesus jesus.

Peter wheeled, looking anxious. She made a sharp intake of breath, the soreness hugging the bone now. Fuck fuck jesus. Then there was another noise. A slow hissing. Shhh. It was Peter saying Shhh.

She looked at him, still clutching the ankle, not sure.

Sshhhh. He looked desperate. For crying out loud, Rachel. All that noise, banging into things.

What? she said.

You're so bloody clumsy. So bloody. He waved an arm limply. I don't know. Can you not be a bit less obvious for once and just. His voice died back, breathless. Just calm down.

Neither of them moved or spoke for a moment.

People are sleeping, he said. His shoulders slumped. Sleeping.

He didn't say anything else. Just clasped the rim of his tee-shirt, hands cupped where his genitals were beneath the cloth before his gaze broke and he looked away.

Rachel straightened up, taking her time. Peter was there on the other side of the bed, his face the colour of separated milk. She looked at his face, the curve of his back. He wasn't well, he was missing sleep. They both were. It wasn't the right time to start asking questions now, be angry or hurt. It wasn't the right time to say she felt the two of them blocked her out all the time and it wasn't just the language: it was the different mealtimes, shut doors when they stayed up in the evenings or worked together, heads close over blueprints and drawings. It was a lot of things. He seemed to be between them all the time. Even now, in the middle of the night changing the sheets in her own bedroom, the bastard wouldn't go away. It was something to do with Marc, this embarrassment of Peter's, his saying she was – what was it? – too obvious. Too *there*, was that what he meant? The time the two of them had gone out to some pub when he arrived, the way Marc smiled when she asked to come too: she wouldn't like it there, it would bore her and she said how can you be sure and he smiled again. He just knew. Now Rachel thought she knew something too. The reason he hung around the house so much, why there was no time they were alone except when she and Peter were in bed and even then he was semi-fucking comatose with sleep or drink, too tired to talk, too tired for anything at all. They hadn't made love since that man had been here. They hadn't even embraced for christsake.

Shhh.

The low insect drone of the fan heater stopped. Completely. Peter had slid back down onto his heels, still shaking, and switched it off. It was impossible to tell if he had silenced her again, if she had imagined it. In the bloom of silence, Rachel looked hard at his back, the skin tight over his spine. This terrible yearning to touch. He wasn't well. He had woken her up saying it, not knowing what to do. And for three nights she'd been fetching sheets and stripping beds because she didn't know what to do either. And still they soaked through. Because it wasn't flu. It wasn't that kind of sickness. It was something between the two of them, something between the two men. She knew she was shaking too now only it didn't show. A bead of sweat glistened on his jaw, melting into stubble as he stood up, facing her. Eye to eye. He would not understand if she touched him now, if she took his face in her hands and kissed him. Hard.

Sorry, he said. Almost inaudible. Sorry.

It wasn't the right time. Not the right time at all. She shrugged, looked down. The sheet was there in her hands. She took a pace back and snapped it wide, a white billow over the mattress. Peter stood up and moved to the other side. Their hands started smoothing then, putting the thing to rights. The Dutchman moaned, turning in his sleep. Rachel and Peter went on making the bed. They would make the bed, go back between its sheets and not sleep. He would sweat. It would not be possible to comfort him because of the burning, his skin burning up and needing peace and calm. Her touch would not allow him peace. It would make him worse. And she would lie next to him, trying not to come too close.

She must have slept, finally, on the edge of her side of the mattress. This cramping in her shoulders, stiffness up the back of her neck. Maybe not well, but she had slept. And still he'd managed to be up first, pulling the curtains, getting on with things. Making breakfast. He laughed then. She heard him laughing, through in the other room. His head tilted, his neck bared. He'd have fixed something for him and Marc, the way he had every morning, not mentioned his waking in the night. When she went through, there would be general jollity and making light of things, gentle protests she was being fussy and over-protective – you know how women are. She heard him laugh again: Marc, his voice rising as he laughed too.

Rachel lay as still. As still as.
Keeping her eyes shut. There was nothing she wanted to see.

It was time to get up.
Time to get up and tell herself not to be difficult. She would tell herself not to be paranoid and get out of bed. She would wash her face with cold water to make it look less hellish and smile when she opened the kitchen door. She wouldn't ask if he'd taken the vitamin C, at least not immediately. After a couple of minutes though, she wouldn't be able to help herself. Very soon now, she would get up, defying lost sleep and godknew what else. She would butter toast, make a joke of

herself dosing him with fizzy health supplements from a wine glass, and smile some more. It was all she could think of to do. Her head crushing tighter. Knowing it wasn't flu.

It wasn't

flu.

proposal

Shit

zeroed through two walls and into her ear, bloomed there like a
bomb.

The way his voice could do that, just find her out: through precast
concrete and pebbledash like a heat-seeking missile, straight through
solid structures. The windows not even open.

Shit

coming closer.

Then the door sprang off its catch and a blur of what had to be
Callum shot by the back of the settee. She knew it had to be Callum
because of the way the air displaced, shifting out his road. Also he
spoke. It's only me jesus crying out loud there's birdshit all over the
fucking car for godsake, before the door slammed back again, him
outside, her in. The reverberation of his voice hung on, palpable.
Irene imagined if she sat very still, screwing her eyes up, she'd be able
to see it: wee lines radiating from the space he had occupied then
abandoned, like in a cartoon. She waited till whatever the lines were
made of melted then got off the settee. It was ok. It was always ok. Just
Callum, that excitable way he got – in the cupboard and out of it
before you even had time to turn round. He would be outside with his

polishing cloth again, quite the thing. She imagined him scouring, lifting the rag with wee daisies he'd made out of an old sheet. He'd lift it up and glare at the wee daisies for not trying hard enough, then press them back down hard, scouring till the windows gave in. Spotless, like they weren't really there. The way he liked them.

Irene? Five minutes ok?

A dunt at the door, feet on gravel, car locks freeing and slamming. He'd have a heart attack before he was thirty at this rate. She was never done telling him and he was never done kidding on he couldn't hear. Irene couldn't blame him. Nagging, you called it; what husbands gave in evidence they were Not Understood when they spoke to strange women in pubs. What they couldn't talk to other men about for fear they'd be thought less of. She lifted the empty glass on the coffee table, looked into it. If she didn't take it through, rinse it now, there would be a ring of dried-out sherry welded onto the bottom when they got back. Everything else was done: cases out, sockets switched off, doors pulled over, the curtain arranged so it looked not shut and not open at the same time. She glanced across at the kitchen, back down at the glass, then raised it, tilting her head back for a last drop that didn't come. What did was a clear picture of the corner of the ceiling. Those marks up there. They were definitely getting worse. Not just dots and maybe-not-there-at-all things but noticeably greynesses, widening out. A piece of wallpaper was lifting from the border as well, something blurry, fungal maybe, creeping out from underneath.

Irene? Cmon. It's now or never.

She put the glass down on the mantelpiece, reached for her bag, draped the strap over one shoulder without taking her eyes off the ceiling. The car horn sounded. Twice. Irene bounced the keys in her hand, still looking up. Then turned her heel quickly and opened the door.

Callum wasn't in the car. He was staring at the guttering and pointing.

Look at that, he said, Look.

The gutter was glutted with chicken bones.

Bloody dogs at the bin bags again, he said. You think folk would feed their own mutts. Look at it. Terrible. He rubbed his hands together and looked up then, smiling. We ready for the off?

Irene looked at him.

We got everything?

Callum, she said. She hoped it sounded irritated.

He looked back, blank. Not playing.

How come knowing whether we've got everything's my area of expertise, exactly? Why's it my responsibility?

His eyebrows had sunk. He hadn't a clue. Irene tilted her head to one side, sighing.

Yes, she said. Yes. We've got everything.

He went back to the smiling, the mild abrasion of his palms. Irene poked her arse and one foot inside the car, keeping her knees as together as possible. The dress rode over her thighs anyway, a pale triangle of knicker showing through the crotch of her tights when she sat down but she said nothing. It was one thing being fed up with the weeness of the MG but another being sarky about it. He was quite right: the so-called witticisms about sports cars and penile length were no longer funny. Besides, the frock wasn't his fault. He might well have suggested she wear the damn thing, said if he had the choice he would wear a dress now and again, but it was her that had put it on. Anyway, dresses were better for you. They didn't give you thrush and compression marks the way jeans did. He was right about that as well.

Hey look, he was saying. He was pointing at the floor. New rugs.

She saw things like red toilet seat surrounds, black letters chasing themselves under her feet. HERS. HERS HERS HERS HERS HERS in an endless loop. Callum's had their own railtrack. HIS HIS HIS HIS HIS.

Two for the price of one, he said. He was turning the ignition and looking over, thrilled to hell. Good eh?

He stroked her leg, laughing, his mouth wide open. Irene couldn't think of the last time she'd seen him in this kind of mood. Laddish. Like a wee boy. It was more than the new rugs, more than the daftness he'd bought them for. He looked over at her then, his eyes shiny: a look that said she was a thing of beauty, a joy for ever. It was the frock. It didn't matter how crabbit she was being, he was loving seeing her in the bloody thing. They were going on holiday and she was wearing a frock. Irene looked at the smile, at Callum behind it.

There's paper coming off the wall in the livingroom, she said. I told you it needed redecorating.

He shook his head in a manner suggestive of astonishment, one side of the smile widening.

I don't know, he said. You're unreal, you. He shook his head again, good-natured, flicked the indicator switch. He laughed out loud. You're un-bloody-real.

Calum's mum was in the kitchen surrounded by smells of spitting meat. Callum ducked to avoid a mobile that hadn't been there before. Lavender bags strung on garden twine, tiny pink bows all down its length.

You've arrived, she said.

No lipstick yet but her nails freshly varnished, pearl-white hearts. Their tips cramped what was left of a cabbage tight against the chopping board, pale green shreds falling in layers to cover the design of little girls in mob caps. She gazed down at the cabbage like the Virgin Mary, keeping slicing. Callum picked a single sliver off the board and held it near his mouth. He always took something when he came in, posed with it till she gave him a mock slap on the wrist so he could do his look of mock outrage. It was a routine. Irene watched them do the whole thing.

When's the dinner ready then? he said. I'm starving.

O you, she said, O you, and rolled her eyes.

There was a recipe for rack of lamb on the pinboard. The cardboard horseshoe with a sprig of heather was coming loose. Cousin Angela's wedding favour. Her eldest must be six by this time, Irene thought. Six at least.

Is he not terrible? Mrs Hamilton said.

Irene asked if there was anything she could do. Mrs Hamilton said she'd give her a shout. It was what she always said. When the shout came, it would be to come and get a basket of bread that was already sliced and carry it through. It was all a shout ever meant. She always asked though. Through the connecting door, the tv was running *Tom and Jerry*. The news would be next. She watched it till the tune started but didn't go through. Callum never liked her doing that. He liked her to stay with them in the kitchen even if there was nothing she was useful for. He was anxious about it now, looking over while pretending to rummage in the cutlery drawer, exclamation marks showing between his eyes. Irene nodded to let him know it was ok. He poked his thumb into the air to show her he was pleased and went back to the rummaging while Mrs Hamilton lifted their jackets, carried them out to the hall cupboard. The soft sound of receding fur mules, Callum crashing out cutlery in fours.

There were two geraniums on the sill: no withered leaves, no fallen blooms. Beyond them, Irene saw Callum's father working, making holes in the dark garden border soil. His hair had been cut, the temples shot with more grey. She watched him reach and ferret forth something from a plastic bag, something with roots that would fit the hollow he had just cleared with his bare hands. Dirty but fine boned, the wrists narrow. They had worked for a security firm for twenty-four years, those hands, gloved in leather: the rest of him swathed in navy, a helmet with a full-face visor. Irene watched him work, forcing his fingers into the soil and wondered if he'd ever battered the hell out of somebody during those twenty-four years; gone queerbashing or studied the reader's wives or Dutch porn the other boys kept stashed under the seats of the van. It was entirely possible. He wouldn't have enjoyed it or anything but it was still entirely possible. He was looking round for something now, failing to see it. He stood up instead, wiping his hands along the seams of the trousers he wore for the garden and would wear to the table too. On the edge of the lawn, she could see a pair of garden gloves, the plastic tie unbroken. The ones she had given him for Christmas. To George xxx. Untouched. He strode over them, careful of plant shoots, heading for the house.

The door opened. Mr Hamilton stood on the top step of his own back door, knocking mud off his boots, a loose lock of hair falling forward over his brow as his feet struck the stone. He nodded to Irene, inscrutable. Callum came back through from the livingroom and opened the fridge door.

Aye aye. He spoke to the freezer compartment.

Aye aye. His father nodded again, eyes focused in the general direction of Callum's feet. All right, then?

Callum looked above the white door rim for a moment, a kind of confused smile coming with him. His face was pink.

Aye fine, he said, the smile stuck. Like he'd been caught doing something naughty. The eyes of the two men met by mistake for a moment before Mrs Hamilton opened the serving hatch. The peach-coloured lipstick she was so fond of, the one that made her mouth look like it had been squeezed out of an icing bag, moved.

You've a clock in that stomach of yours, it said. ESP or something.

George bashed his foot one last time for luck and closed the back door. What is it then? he said. He didn't look at her.

I don't care what it is, Callum said. Just get it on the table.

Mrs Hamilton looked at them. She looked at Irene. I don't know, she said. Her face plump with happiness, delight even. The things you've to put up with in this house.

Mr Hamilton started washing his hands.

It was cabbage, potatoes, cauliflower and carrots. The basket of bread went in the middle: the big plate of roast something, last. The roast always sat next to George because George always carved it. It was George's job. He cut the meat and put it onto plates. Irene's was always first. She took her plate, told him it was fine. Callum took his, looked down at the meat and said, We're going to Belfast.

Silence. Irene looked. She knew from the way the words were hanging over the dinner. The bugger hadn't told them. He'd said he would and he hadn't. It was the first he was telling them now. Mrs Hamilton looked at George, looked away again, held a big spoon of carrots out for general inspection.

Your daddy grew these. What do you think?

Very nice, Callum said. Lovely.

Irene wondered when the fork would come over. Callum usually pinched her meat and gave her his vegetables. He did it particularly when he was trying to be charming. The fork didn't come though. She heard George put down his knife, the silence stiffen up.

When? He said it very slowly. When's this then?

Callum kept his eyes on the salt shaker, poking it as if the holes were blocked. He shoogled it a couple of times.

Soon, he said.

Oh yes. You're going to Belfast, then. Soon.

Callum put the shaker down. Mrs Hamilton settled back.

Everybody got everything they want?

When's that then, George said. Soon? What's that supposed to mean? What for?

Soon. Irene knew from the way he said it he was looking at her, wanting her to look back. Soon, ok? Soon.

He chewed something as though it was burning his mouth, swallowed.

Soon, he said. Tomorrow.

George looked straight at Callum then back at his plate. His mother doled out cabbage.

For goodness' sake, she said.

Callum ran his finger along the blunt edge of the knife, back again. He didn't look at her.

You never tell us nothing, she said. It's terrible. Is it a holiday or what? It's terrible.

George made a noise like clearing catarrh and swallowed.

You could have stayed at your auntie Pat's if you'd let us know. I don't suppose you've contacted her either. Eh? Contacted Pat?

Not yet.

Ha. There was a note of genuine pleasure in George's voice, triumph or something. Irene heard it. Not yet he says ha. I didn't think so. Not yet eh? Ha!

His knife scraped against the white ceramic.

Stupid, spending money. You could have stayed at Pat's. Dunno what's wrong with you, boy. Got secrecy like a disease. He sniffed. I'm taking it on trust you know what you're doing, boy.

Callum.

His mother's eyebrows had collapsed like a swing bridge. Not holding bowls or spoons any more, she looked bereft, lonely. Even her back slumped.

Honest, it's terrible. If you're away a holiday you could just say. I don't know what you're like that for, son. She looked like somebody had punched her.

You'll miss the big meeting as well, George said. He mumbled. You won't be here.

Not even saying, though. She looked at her husband. He was

202

cutting a potato. You'd think we were bad to him or something. You'd think we were – then she couldn't think what else they might be and stopped. Irene looked at Mrs Hamilton, the way she tried to meet the gaze of people who would not look back. For six years she had been calling her Mrs Hamilton. Now, suddenly, she wanted to call her something else.

The carrots, she said.

Callum turned. They all did.

These carrots here. They're very nice. Wilma.

Everyone had stopped eating, nonplussed. Then George's face melted.

Course they are, he said. Grew them out there. Organic what-you-call-it. Organic methods. Good for you.

His teeth, clean marble slates, showed briefly. He'd never had a filling in his life. Wilma held out the blue dish still half-full of orange discs.

Here. Her voice was full of something. Have some more, she said. There's plenty.

Belfast, George said. I don't know. But it was better somehow. It was definitely better. Callum raised his eyebrows so only Irene could see, keeping his head down while he slipped his fork over and stole the last slice of her meat.

Oh you, his mother said. Under the peach-coloured smile, the real colour of her lips beginning to show. Oh you.

There was the eating of pudding, the clearing away, the settling of dishes in the sink.

No don't you do them, she said. Away you two through and watch tv.

Singing came through the hatch with the water noises, wee bits of ABBA and godknew. George went to get his roses done before the sky

203

clouded over. Irene and Callum had two cups of tea, a Hitchcock remake and *Songs of Praise*. The usual Sunday afternoon.

George missed the chips and cold meat and Callum doing the washing up. Callum went out to the shed to fetch him in when they were leaving. They all stood on the front door step except Irene. There wasn't room for four. Mother and son kissed, she on her toes, fingers tipping his shoulders as if she might keel over reaching so high. Father and son didn't. They didn't touch at all. George came down the step for Irene though. He leaned forward, brushed her cheek with his mouth pursed. Nice in that frock, he said. Should wear a frock more often. Then he stood back and smiled. He had a beautiful smile, George. They both had beautiful smiles. Callum looked like both of them whether he smiled or not. You could see it without even trying.

You taking that thing? George pointed at the car. You serviced it then?

Callum got in, rolled the window down. It's fine, dad.

Fine for a heap of junk. Bet it won't start first time.

It did. Callum stuck his head out the window, triumphant. His father smiled again: unstinting, clean. He waved.

See and have a nice time, Wilma shouted. She waved too. George and Wilma smiling on the front porch, forearms ticking like metronomes. They kept doing it till the car was out of sight. Callum relaxed into the driving seat, changed gear.

Heep of junk, he said. Cheeky bastard.

Three EXPECT DELAYS signs were evenly spaced along the approach to the shore road. The shore road was usually ok. Sunday nights it was hardly ever busy at all. Tonight it was a risk. Callum took it anyway. He weighed the possibilities and made a decision. After ten minutes or so with no trouble, he relaxed. Irene didn't realise till he did it he'd been anything else. He put his hand on her leg, patting it lightly.

Ok?

Irene said nothing.

The patting became a long stroke, knee to thigh, back down to rest where it started.

What time we due at your mother's then?

Ten.

She knows we're coming?

Of course she knows. I told her not to make up the spare room. Told her we'd do it.

Callum's hand cut off at the wrist by the black jersey, white against the orange tights. Irene stared at it.

Callum, she said. She paused, choosing the right words, the moment. How come you never said to your folks about us going away? The hand moved back to the steering wheel. He looked in the rear-view mirror, back out front again, checking something. He checked it for ages.

Callum I'm asking you a question.

I did tell them. They must have forgot.

Irene levelled her eyes on his face. Callum. You didn't tell them.

I did.

No you didn't.

I did.

Irene sighed. Callum blushed right down to his neck.

I did. They must have forgot. Honest.

Callum. She bent his name into a hillock. He looked at her out the corner of an eye and sighed.

Ok ok, he said. Ok so I didn't tell them. I own up it's a fair cop guv I'll never do it again. Satisfied?

No I'm not satisfied. I know perfectly well you didn't tell them. I don't want to know *whether*, Callum. I want to know *why*. *Why* didn't you tell them?

He drove, staring hard at the road. His chin disappeared.

I just didn't want any hassle.

What hassle?

The twenty questions thing. You know what he's like about the car, telling me what I should be doing and all that stuff. You know what he's like, Irene.

You could have told your mother. Her voice was down to its usual octave again, coaxing. Cmon. You could have said to her on the phone.

He sighed again.

There was nothing stopping you.

What difference does it make eh? It's ok now. They weren't bothered.

They were so bothered. More to the point I was bothered. Me, Callum. *I* was bothered.

Aw cmon Irene.

Cmon nothing. I *was*. They must think I'm a rude bastard, that I was in on it or something.

In on it? In on what for godsake? I'm twenty-two for christsake Irene: I don't need to tell my father everything I bloody do. Am I supposed to be asking for permission or something, is that it?

That's a complete side-issue, Callum, *completely* beside-the-point. The point is not about asking permission: the point is you told me you *did* and you bloody *hadn't*. You *hadn't*.

So?

So you gave me misinformation. You made me look like an idiot and/or an accomplice and I don't like it.

Oh for fucksake Irene.

Don't fucksake me, Callum. You did. Either they thought I was in on not telling them, on not giving a toss what they thought *or* they've picked up the fact you never tell me what's going on half the time either. I don't like it. I don't like not being told what's going on. It's embarrassing.

Callum snorted.

It is. It's humiliating. I don't like being shown up in front of folk like that. Especially not your parents. It's controlling and humiliating and I feel belittled by it.

Belittled. He said it like it was a foreign word. Belittled?

The car was slowing down, tacking behind a queue of others. Yellow lights were flashing up ahead somewhere. Callum pulled up the handbrake. The creaking died away.

That's ridiculous, Irene. That's the most ridiculous thing I ever heard.

No it isn't.

Yes. It. Is.

Irene turned to the side window. Outside was getting dark now, the sea washing with nothing to glitter off. She watched it come and go in the half-light, mist gathering in the corners of the window.

I don't know why you're doing this.

It was a very measured voice. She turned round. Callum was shaking his head, holding the wheel with both hands. The car was rolling, almost imperceptibly.

Oh for godsake. She sighed. Are we going to play a you-started-it game?

Silence. Big silence.

Look. Irene breathed heavily down her nose, rubbed her temples hard. Ok. I'm doing this badly. What I'm really trying to say is you don't need to be so . . . whatever it is.

I don't need to be so what?

Manipulative, Callum. That's what you don't need to be. Telling lies about trivial wee things then getting annoyed when I find out. Like I'm not supposed to let on I've noticed.

He pulled the brake back on full, his mouth set.

Me. *I* tell *you* lies? I tell you *lies*?

Ok maybe it's not lies. Evasions then. Is that a less contentious word-choice?

He said nothing for a moment, just glared at the windscreen. Sometimes. He said it like the first number in a countdown. Sometimes, Irene, you can be a sarcastic cow.

That's as may be, she said. But you're still doing it. You're avoiding the issue, steering the conversation away from what I'm trying to say.

Which is?

Which is – her voice was getting louder again, hard to keep control of – which is, Callum, you telling me you'd told your folks when you hadn't. The issue is you controlling information and not telling the truth.

I do tell you the truth.

You tell me the truth?

Yes. I do.

Ok. You tell me the truth, then. Tell me it now. I'd like the truth about this meeting, please.

What meeting?

This meeting you won't be there for. Tell me about that.

Callum said nothing.

That's all I know, there's some meeting and you won't be there – and I only know *that* because your dad said, only there was other stuff going on at the time. Now there isn't so you can tell me. What meeting? On you go.

I don't know. I don't know what he was talking about.

Irene looked at him. She kept looking at him. Callum intensified his gaze on the nothing that was behind the windscreen.

Are you being serious? she said.

Eh? He screwed his face up as though something was annoying him, as though he was concentrating really hard and not able to hear her. Eh?

I said –

Callum sounded the horn suddenly, leaning hard on the middle of the steering wheel.

Look at this carry on, he said. Look. Bloody road works eh?

Irene turned away. She banged her head off the side window. Then she did it again. I give up, she said. She exhaled very slowly. I. Bang. Give. Bang. Up. Bang.

Her hair had brushed a gap in the condensation. Through the streaky mesh, she could see the shore wall still there, the mission rock behind it. ETERNITY. She could see it quite clearly: the paint luminous at this time of night. Nothing else, not even the sea. Just the rock and its message, a present from the holy rollers who prowled the seafront with a bucket of whitewash every summer. They had cookouts and things, sang hymns. ETERNITY. Irene looked at the letters, the gaps between them. She was wondering how often they did it, repainting the same thing to keep it clear, whether they came at night to keep the whole thing a kind of mystery. Maybe you were meant to think god had done it, or something. Then it clicked. George saying All right? that way, Callum going coy. The conversations she'd heard father and son having umpteen times and thought were just one-sided. It clicked.

You've joined the Lodge, haven't you? she said. You've joined the bloody Orange Lodge.

She turned and looked at him. He was looking back at her, his face flushed.

No wonder you're fucking embarrassed. She was staring at him so hard her eyes hurt. Christ on wheels Callum. The Orange Lodge.

Callum's mouth was open but nothing was coming out. He

looked caught. Scared. Ridiculous. For no reason, without seeming to want to, Irene started laughing. A steady through-the-nose snort. Callum looked away quickly, crunching into the wrong gear, back out again. The car in front had started moving. Callum let the motor inch forward, closing the gap carefully but the engine was revving. Irene didn't drive but she knew it didn't need to rev that hard. The laugh had died away now, stopped as fast as it had come. A string of red lights flashed on down the whole slope of the hill. The car settled on its hunkers again, rocking slightly.

He was still saying nothing, just sniffing. After a moment he made little coughing sounds, sniffing some more.

Jesus christ almighty, she said. She didn't turn round, just kept staring down. The pattern on the frock rose and fell with her breathing, rose and fell. She watched it, waiting. Then looked up. His eyes were very shiny, trained on the tail-lights ahead.

Dad put my name up, he said. I thought I could do something he'd like for a change. That's all. Doesn't matter.

He rubbed the bridge of his nose, wiped one side of his face with the back of his hand. The other held on to the steering wheel. It held on tight. The insides of the windows were steaming up again. The car was completely still.

What are we doing, Irene?

His voice was so soft, she hoped for a moment he hadn't spoken at all. He had though. She said nothing waiting.

Everything, he said. Everything is up in the air all the fucking time. Can't even visit my parents these days without something, some bloody thing . . .

He ran out of words and leaned forward on the steering wheel.

Look. I wasn't trying to keep things from you. Honest. I'm not trying to do anything, just get on with a normal life. That's all I want. I want us to have a normal life for godsake. You and me. That's all I'm trying to do.

210

And all I want is to be let in on things. I want you to stop making decisions for me.

He sat up again, glared at her.

It's still the engagement ring isn't it?

Irene said nothing.

You just can't let it go, can you?

Irene said nothing.

Ok, he said. I confess, I confess. I did a terrible thing: I bought you an engagement ring. Yes, I know I should have asked you first. I know I shouldn't have told anybody we were getting married before I asked you either. I know I know. I said I was sorry. Most women would have managed to find something flattering about it but there you go. I have to say I'm sorry. So I did. And I am. And I'm still getting this shit.

Irene said nothing.

Jesus christ Irene, what are you wanting me to do though? I don't go on about what you've done. That affair you had, that bloody John guy or whatever his name was. I don't keep dragging that up. I've tried to put it behind me. We need to put in a bit of effort for christsake, move forward. You don't fucking try.

Irene said nothing.

What are you thinking?

Nothing.

I know what I think.

Nothing.

I think we should get married.

This time she groaned. He just kept going.

I've asked you often enough. If we got married things would be different, all sorts of things. You'd see.

The engine purring, a stink of damp dog. Looking down, the short blue hem, her legs swathed in orange mesh. Tights. She was wearing tights because. Because. The words HERS HERS HERS coursing under her feet. She could think of nothing to say.

Please. His voice was clear and sure. All you need to do is show willing, Irene. That's all.

He swallowed, didn't look at her.

I don't want us to go off the rails again.

After a while the car in front started to pull away, this time more definitely. Callum reached for the glove compartment, took out the cloth and wiped the inside of the windscreen clear. Irene took it from him, their fingers touching briefly, and finished the rest. It was her job anyway. Slowly, he released the handbrake. Callum's big, competent hands. Like George's. Just like his dad's.

What time did you say we were due at your mother's then? he said.

The side-window showed nothing. Irene rolled it down, watching the glass level fall, breathing deep. Ozone and pitch black. That's all there was. The sea was out there somewhere but only in theory. There was nothing of it visible at all. She had a notion for a moment to ask him to stop, pull the car over so they could go outside, walk for a bit on the sand. But the line was moving. They were inside Callum's car going to her mother's to spend the night ready for the morning ferry. She'd be waiting for them now, watching tv and wondering where they'd got to, nipping in to check the big bed with the top sheet turned back. Everything would be waiting. Irene tucked the cloth away where it belonged, spoke to the windscreen.

I told you already, she said. Ten. She's expecting us at ten.

We're going to be late, he said.

Ahead, the motorway lights, official apologies on reflective metal. Cars picking up speed.

six horses

1

Eve is reading.

After three days' climbing, they still did not know each other's
names. Eve sees two people, a man and a woman, peering over the
edges of scarves, mouths muffled against rock dust. In this way, dusk
falling, they became separated from the rest of the party. Speechless,
unsure of their bearings, they climbed deeper hoping to hear an echo
of the others from a nearby chamber. Eventually, they reached a soft
place in the rock, a shelf already giving under their boots: crumbs of
shale and pebbles at first, then the ground dissolving, separating from
itself with such languor neither of them thought to move out of its
way. A light ripping sound of fibres parting, and they fell, not far, into a
narrow tunnel underground. A fine deposit gusting up from the floor,
twisting in the light of their helmets like smoke and filling their nostrils
with a taint like gunpowder; acrid, dry. The walls shone dimly with
hematite and coal. Thrown together, listening, they waited till the dust
settled back around their feet. Then, soundless lest the vibrations
disturb the rock overhead, began walking. After only a short distance,
the roof angled sharply downwards. They could no longer stand
upright but kept going. At the end of the tunnel, they found a tumulus,
a swollen belly in the wall covered with lichen. He ran his palm over it,

found it warm. The texture of dried peat blocks or matted earth. They exchanged glances only once then began, pulling with bare hands till the bulge opened suddenly, a hole big enough for the lamps of their helmets to shine through. Inside, spectral in the white beams, they saw a horse. A horse whole and standing in a sealed tomb. The man couldn't help himself. He stretched his hand. One touch. And the beast was no longer there. Vanished, crumbled to powder. It was no longer there. He is glad she (he puts his mud-caked hand inside hers, squeezes tight) was with him or he might have thought the whole thing a dream. Eve reads the scientific explanation, an irrelevance. What matters is only this: a man and a woman looked at nothing with a faint trail of smoke through it, a roomful of mist where a horse had been, then looked at each other. Knowing they would never be strangers again. Eve clutches the paper like hair, looks across the room.

2

Listening, the timbers of an unread book creaking under his hands, he keeps his eyes steady. The headphones, she knows, are not to keep the sound in; they are to keep it out. If she listens hard she can hear music but it's distant, an echo. On the other side of the street, workmen are scaling scaffolding. Behind his back, they lean against the monkey bars, peer across to see if she is watching. His book falls, unnoticed, from his lap. A boy in a yellow helmet, a tattoo of Pegasus winding round one arm, hangs smiling by his boots from the sky.

3

Another cigarette. He lights up, draws; the tips of his fingers amber. He picks winners while she picks up the phone. There is no-one at the other side. She'd rather go home tonight, she says. Tonight she won't stay. Cab and a train, he says. This is serious. Smoke trails over his lower lip, spills over the newsprint picture: its black and white eyes, the bit between its teeth.

4

The tunnel goes on. Blackness hurling past the window, reflecting her features on smeary glass. People don't die for lack of love, she thinks: at least no-one dies. Except children. She looks at the eyes in the window pretending to belong to someone else. For a split-second, she sees what he sees: a woman with an alien face flaring on the tunnel wall before it gives way. The wall disappears taking her with it and the tunnel is over, past. Her ears fill with quiet as a rabbit makes a ghost of itself against the scrub. Closer to, a luminous shape rears out of the wash of grey. Grazing.

5

It is the room she left but not the same. Still cold, but tiny things look warm, look open to touch. That someone else could be here did not seem impossible any more. It's all right, she would tell him. We're not children. He wouldn't be listening. He would be looking at her. Dark-drown eyes. Outside, past the advertising hoardings, the washed shore wall, white horses rising on the crests of harbour waves

6

They have not had too much to drink. He takes off his shirt, his shoes; loosens his belt. The last layer. Thick twine over his sternum and belly widens out into black ferns, an upturned V at his crotch. His penis is so pale in the half-light she can't help her mouth being drawn like a butterfly, a moth. She has only known fair men, has not been prepared for this dark texture, this hardness, the scent of this skin. She wonders till his hand stretches for her hair, then stops wondering altogether. Eve, he says. He says her name. In the morning, she finds five long strands from his head, a cache of pubic crescents, a single eyelash. Faint trails on the white cotton streaked with a henna of coming menstrual blood. It is the room he left but not the same. Her head is full of rockfalls, coal-dust phosphorescence, melting horses.